MISERY GUTS
and WORRY WARTS

Born in the UK, Morris Gleitzman emigrated to Australia with his family at the age of sixteen. His career took off as a screenwriter and a newspaper columnist before he became a successful author. He has written a number of children's books, including *Two Weeks with the Queen*, *Blabber Mouth*, *Sticky Beak* and *Belly Flop*. He lives in Melbourne and has two children.

The BBC television series of *Misery Guts* was filmed in Australia, on the beautiful Queensland coast. It was adapted for the screen by Mary Morris, who wrote the scripts for all thirteen episodes, and who also dramatised *Two Weeks with the Queen* and *Blabber Mouth* for the theatre. *Blabber Mouth* and *Sticky Beak* have also been adapted for television, and the programme, made for Channel Four, won an International Emmy award in November 1998.

D0271044

Morris Gleitzman

Misery Guts

and

Worry Warts

Illustrated by John Levers

MACMILLAN CHILDREN'S BOOKS

Misery Guts first published 1991 by Blackie and Sons Ltd
Worry Warts first published 1992 by Blackie Children's Books
This double volume first published 1999 by Macmillan Children's Books
a division of Macmillan Publishers Limited
25 Eccleston Place, London SW1W 9NF
and Basingstoke

Associated companies throughout the world

ISBN 0 330 39103 8

Text copyright © Morris Gleitzman 1991, 1992
Illustrations copyright © John Levers 1991, 1992

The right of Morris Gleitzman to be identified as the
author of this work has been asserted by him in accordance
with the Copyright, Designs and Patents Act 1988.

3 5 7 9 8 6 4 2

A CIP catalogue record for this book is available from
the British Library.

Printed and bound in Great Britain by Mackays of Chatham plc, Kent

MISERY GUTS

For my parents

ONE

Keith's heart was pounding.

Calm down, he thought. You're not robbing a bank. You're not kidnapping anybody. You're just painting a fish and chip shop orange.

He looked up and down his street, peering into the early morning fog.

Everything was grey. Grey houses. Grey shops. Grey cars. Grey blocks of flats looming up into a grey sky.

The cold air was making his ears hurt.

This is why, he thought. This is why Mum and Dad are such misery guts. The weather.

He pulled his collar up round his ears. Thirty-five years of it was enough to give anyone a long face. He'd only had twelve and a quarter years of it and even he got the willies sometimes.

Oh well, he told himself, they'll be feeling better soon. When they see what I've done.

He looked at his watch. Seven-fifteen. Mum'll be awake soon. Dad'll be back from the market at eight.

And neither of them's got a clue they're about to be cheered up.

Keith grinned at the thought.

Then he turned back to the shop front, dipped his brush into the tin and carried on painting.

The Tropical Mango Hi-Gloss spread over the dull brown of the window frame like liquid sunshine.

Keith's heart pounded faster. It looked even better than he'd thought it would.

While he painted, he imagined Mum and Dad's faces when they saw it. The big grins spreading over both their faces. Those big droopy creases at the corners of Dad's mouth, gone. Those frown lines on Mum's forehead, vanished.

He stood on a soft-drink crate to reach the top bit of the window frame, brushing the Tropical Mango on as thickly as he could so none of the brown showed through. When they see this, thought Keith, they'll think the sun's come out.

Then he heard the sound of a door slamming. He looked round. It wasn't the sun coming out, it was Mr Naylor from next door.

Keith sighed. Here we go.

Mr Naylor looked at the paint, at the brush, and at the Tropical Mango window frame.

'What are you doing?' he asked suspiciously.

Teaching sheep to juggle toasters, thought Keith, then remembered he'd promised Mum he wouldn't be cheeky to Mr Naylor now he was twelve.

'Painting our shop. For Dad's birthday. It's a surprise.'

Mr Naylor gave the window frame a long stare.

'Won't dry in this weather,' he said.

'It's quick-drying,' said Keith. 'You get a brilliant,

long-lasting finish in only hours. Says so on the tin.'

'Horrible colour,' said Mr Naylor.

'The man in the shop said orange reminds people of their summer holidays,' said Keith.

'It's dripping on the pavement,' said Mr Naylor and shuffled away towards the bus stop.

Keith wondered when Mr Naylor had last smiled. 1847 probably.

He looked at the pavement. There were a few orange spots. He rubbed them with his foot, but they were already starting to go like old custard skin. Oh well, he thought, what's a bit of spotty pavement when you're bringing happiness to two people.

He moved on to the door. It was good to have a decent-sized flat bit to work on. He'd gone a bit wonky on the window frame in places.

He smoothed big brushfuls of paint on and had a vision of Mum and Dad, big grins still on their faces, going over to Lewisham and buying themselves some colourful clothes and coming back and having a party for Dad's birthday. Just the three of them. Getting out all their old records, the Rolling Stones and stuff. Mum and Dad dancing. He'd never seen them dance.

The shop door glowed and so did Keith.

A hand reached past him and stuck a rolled-up newspaper in the letter-box.

'Waste of time, that.'

Keith sighed.

Mitch Wilson stepped round him and stuffed a paper into Mr Naylor's letter-box.

'Be filthy dirty in a week.'

'Comes up like new with a simple wipe,' said Keith. 'Says so on telly.'

Tragic, he thought, watching Mitch trying to stuff a wad of magazines through the door of the hairdressers two doors down. Only ten and he was as big a moaner as Mrs Wall in the launderette. She didn't even like people getting married in case the tablecloths from the reception put a strain on her dryers.

'Be filthy dirty again in another week.'

Keith didn't bother answering. No point with a moaner. And only two years ago Mitch Wilson had been an eager little kid who'd wanted to be a Mars Bar salesman.

Keith put the soft-drink crate on top of the dustbin and climbed up to do the sign over the window. Vin's Fish Supplies. He decided to do the background rather than the lettering. Do the lettering in Rain Forest Green later.

As he slapped the paint on, he wondered if there was an award for the Brightest Fish and Chip Shop in Britain. That'd really get Dad's eyes sparkling again. Princess Di dropping in to shake his hand and give him a solid silver cod fillet.

This thought was shattered by a whine.

Keith sighed.

Owen the milkman.

The whine was coming from the milk float but Owen soon started one of his own.

'That's not a colour I'd have chosen, Keith. Show the dirt something awful, bright colours. Won't dry this time of year neither, gloss paint. Wife's cousin did their garage in November, still tacky in March. Tell your mum no yoghurt till Thursday.'

Owen's whine stopped, the float's started and he was gone.

No wonder Mum and Dad are depressed, thought Keith, with a milkman like that.

He finished off the sign and climbed down to get the full effect.

On the pavement he tried to imagine he was a depressed parent. He looked up at the glowing Tropical Mango and felt cheered up immediately. Then he half-closed his eyes and banged himself on the head with his knuckles to see what it would look like with temporary bad eyesight due to a tension headache.

Not bad.

'Keith, what are you doing out here?'

Keith opened his eyes. Mum was standing next to him in her dressing-gown, staring at the Tropical Mango. She stared at it for quite a long time. The frown lines on her forehead looked deeper than ever.

Keith, heart pounding, waited for her to be cheered up.

Instead she stared at him.

'It's a birthday surprise for Dad,' he explained. 'And you.'

He wished she'd stop staring at him.

'Even though it's not your birthday,' he added.

Please smile, Mum, he thought. Please don't turn into Mr Naylor.

'It's to cheer you both up.'

She didn't smile.

11

She stared back at the paint.

She closed her eyes and held them closed for ages.

Must be the paint fumes, he thought. Funny though, they didn't sting my eyes.

She looked at him again.

'Keith.'

Her voice sounded funny. Could paint fumes affect the vocal chords?

'Where did you get the paint?'

'Sally Prescott gave me eleven quid for my stamp collection.'

She breathed out slowly and her face softened a bit.

At last.

But she still didn't smile.

'Keith,' she said, 'I don't think you should be around when Dad gets back.'

Keith was confused. Surely she wasn't planning to pinch the birthday surprise? Pretend it was from her? Not Mum. Not the woman who'd sat up with him all night after he'd seen *Nightmare on Elm Street*.

Before he could tell her he'd go fifty fifty and that was his final offer, Dad came round the corner in the van and pulled up in front of the shop.

Keith stepped forward.

'Happy birthday, Dad. From me and Mum.'

Dad sat behind the wheel, motionless, staring up at the shop, mouth open.

Keith opened the van door in case the surprise had sapped Dad's strength.

'Vin,' said Mum, 'before you say anything, Keith's done this as a birthday present. Just try and remember that, love, he did it as a birthday present.'

All right, Mum, thought Keith, don't overdo it, I think he's got the message.

He waited for Dad to take it all in. For Dad's face to light up with the sheer joy of the Tropical Mango Hi-Gloss. And then for him to throw back his head and roar with delighted laughter.

Or even just give a big grin, like he did in that photo when he won Best Fish and Chips at the Woolwich Show before Keith was born.

Or a smile.

Half a smile.

Keith realised Dad was staring down at the pavement.

Then he looked at Keith with an expression that made Mr Naylor, Mitch Wilson and Owen the milkman look like the happiest people on earth.

'Inside,' he said.

TWO

'It's got to stop, Keith.'

Keith stared at the back of the cornflakes box on the kitchen table. A happy mum, a happy dad and a happy kid were all playing happily with an inflatable beach ball they'd got by sending in two box tops and £4.99.

'Did you hear what I said?' demanded Dad. 'It's got to stop.'

Keith looked up at Dad's face. Dad's mouth was droopier than ever.

He looked up at Mum's face. Her forehead looked like she'd put some tucks in it with the sewing machine.

Keith sighed. They looked like they'd sent in two box tops and £4.99 and got back an inflatable dog poo.

'I'm just trying to cheer you both up,' he said.

'Well it's not working,' said Dad.

Keith wondered if the *Guinness Book Of Records* had a category for The Most Incredibly Obvious Statement Ever Made.

'That business a few weeks ago,' continued Dad. 'Did you honestly think drawing funny faces on the cod fillets with tomato sauce was going to make us dance with joy?'

Not dance with joy, thought Keith. Have a bit of a giggle perhaps.

'Mrs Wall nearly had a heart attack,' said Mum. 'She thought we'd left the heads on them.'

'And rigging up the record player under our bed,' said Dad. 'Me and Mum might be strange, but having the living daylights scared out of us doesn't leave us feeling very cheerful.'

'I thought you liked the Rolling Stones,' said Keith.

'Not at six o'clock in the morning,' said Mum, 'and not that loud. Mr Naylor thought the fryer in the shop had exploded.'

'And now this,' said Dad. 'It's . . . it's . . .'

Keith watched him trying to find the words, pacing around the kitchen.

All right, thought Keith, it's not the best paint job in the world, but it's not bad considering. If Picasso had done his painting in the freezing cold without gloves he'd have dripped a bit and gone over the edges too.

Dad turned to face him.

'Why?' he said. 'That's what I don't understand. Why this obsession with cheering us up?'

'It's not as if we're in mourning or anything,' said Mum. 'Nobody's died. We haven't been robbed. The shop hasn't burnt down.'

'So why all this nonsense about cheering us up,' said Dad. 'Just answer me that. Why?'

* * *

16

First period at school was science and Keith managed to have a quiet word with Mr Crouch the science teacher.

'Sir,' said Keith, 'you know all those science magazines you read, what's the latest research data on cheerful people who have to live with misery guts?'

Mr Crouch, who was reading a gardening magazine, looked at him suspiciously.

'How do you mean?'

'Well,' said Keith, 'if a person who's still pretty cheerful has to live with people who aren't cheerful any more, what's the average amount of time it takes for the cheerful person to end up a misery guts too?'

Mr Crouch told him to go back to his seat and finish boiling his tapwater.

At lunch-time Keith managed to have another quiet word with Mr Crouch.

'Sir, you know how we've just been boiling up tapwater to find the impurities and stuff?'

'Distillation,' said Mr Crouch through a mouthful of peanut butter sandwich. 'It's in your textbook.'

'I was just wondering, sir,' said Keith, 'if there's been any research done on whether impurities in tapwater can turn people into misery guts.'

'Go away,' said Mr Crouch, turning the page of his rose catalogue, 'I'm busy.'

'How about rays from the TV?' said Keith. 'I read somewhere once that TVs give out rays that can make people depressed if they're not getting enough sleep. Either that or microwave ovens.'

Mr Crouch put down his catalogue and his sandwich, stood up, gripped Keith by the shoulder and steered him across the staff room and out into the corridor. Then he went back into the staff room and closed the door.

Keith put his mouth to the keyhole.

'How about the greenhouse effect?'

It was still foggy when Keith walked home from school, but as he turned the corner into his street he could see the Tropical Mango glowing through the fog even at that distance.

He felt a tingle of pleasure.

If it can make me feel good at fifty yards, he thought, it's got to work on them at less than ten feet.

He hurried home to see if Mum and Dad were smiling yet.

They were waiting for him in the shop.

They weren't smiling.

'Son,' said Dad, 'we've decided the time's come to tell you what's what.'

Eh? thought Keith. What does he mean?

It couldn't be where baby cod come from, they'd done that ages ago.

'You're right, Keith,' said Mum, 'me and Dad aren't the happy-go-lucky people we used to be.'

'And there are reasons for that,' said Dad, 'and we want you to know what they are. So you'll stop all this nonsense.'

Keith's insides felt as though they'd just dropped several hundred feet into a bowl of cold batter.

What were they going to tell him? What awful things didn't he know about?

He stared at Mum and Dad, hardly daring to look for the tell-tale signs of brain tumours or fatal diseases you could get from handling too much raw fish.

Dad lifted a big sack of flour onto the counter. And a big drum of fat. He didn't look as if he was suffering from anything too bad.

'Do you know what this is?' he asked.

Keith nodded. 'Fat and flour.'

Dad lifted a sack of potatoes onto the counter and took a block of fish from the freezer.

'And this?'

Oh no, thought Keith, don't tell me Dad's banged his head on the fryer hood and forgotten the basic ingredients of fish and chips.

'Fish and potatoes,' he said. 'The potatoes are the round ones.'

'Not just any fat and flour and fish and potatoes,' said Dad. 'Cheap fat and cheap flour and cheap fish and cheap potatoes.'

Keith realised with a shock there was a wobble in Dad's voice.

'The sort of fat and flour and fish and potatoes I said I'd never use. When I started this shop, before you were born, I only used the best vegetable oil and the best matzo flour and the freshest fish and the best potatoes. I used to turn out the best fish and chips in South London. I don't anymore and that's why I don't spend much time cracking jokes and kicking up my heels.'

Before Keith could ask Dad why he didn't cheer himself up by going back to turning out the best fish and chips in South London, Mum and Dad were steering him up the stairs and into the flat.

They stopped in the little hallway that ran between his bedroom and Mum and Dad's bedroom.

'When we got married,' said Mum, 'me and Dad had wonderful plans. We were going to live here for a few years, and have you, which we did, and then buy a house, and then have a little brother or sister for you.'

Keith stared at her. How many times when he was a kid, when he still said his prayers, had he asked God for a brother or sister? Fifty at least. Almost as many times as he'd asked for a helicopter.

'Why didn't you?' he asked. Now the wobble was in his voice.

Mum took a deep breath. Keith noticed she was squeezing Dad's hand very hard.

'Because we couldn't afford to, love. The shop wasn't earning us enough money.'

'It would have done if Dad had kept on turning out the best fish and chips in South London,' said Keith, turning to Dad. 'Wouldn't it?'

'When we started the shop,' said Dad, 'there was us and one curry place down the street. Now there's us and three curry places and McDonalds and Kentucky Fried and Spud-U-Like and the pub bistro and two other fish and chip shops.'

'The only way we can make a living is to keep our prices down,' said Mum. 'And cheap prices means

cheap ingredients. And no money left over for houses.'
She bit her lip.

Keith frowned.

'But we sell loads of fish and chips, mountains of it.
There must be enough money to rent a house at least.'

Dad looked at him grimly.

'Life's not that simple, son. There's tax and elec-
tricity bills and repairs to the shop and repairs to the
fryers and repayments on the new fridge and insurance
in case Mrs Wall slips in a puddle of vinegar and
council fees and government fees and every time
there's a flood anywhere the price of potatoes goes
through the roof.'

Keith looked at Dad. No wonder his mouth was
droopy.

He looked at Mum. No wonder her forehead looked
like Aunty Joyce's peasant smock party dress.

Then Dad gripped him by both shoulders.

'I'm afraid that life,' said Dad, 'is not a lot of fun.'

'So, love,' said Mum, 'do you understand now?'

'Yes,' said Keith.

THREE

Keith lay in bed planning his next move.

He thought about digging up the pavement outside the shop and planting daffodils. Everyone liked daffs. Even people who didn't like Tropical Mango Hi-Gloss. Even Mum and Dad.

The council wouldn't though.

He had a vision of a council bulldozer arriving and bulldozing all the daffs and him having to jump onto the bulldozer driver from the kitchen window and wrestle him to the ground and . . .

Scrap that idea.

OK, what about a holiday? A camping trip. Borrow Uncle Derek's tent. Go somewhere exotic. Dennis Baldwin and his parents went to Dorset last year. Dad could visit all the Dorset fish and chip shops and make some pen pals.

Keith started working out how long it would take him to earn enough for a camping holiday in Dorset.

He'd just calculated that the 2p a potato Mum and Dad paid him meant he'd have to peel at least ten thousand potatoes, when he remembered that Dennis Baldwin had come home from Dorset six days early last year because his mum had hit his dad over the head with a deckchair.

Scrap that idea.

I know, he thought, I'll ring up a circus and invite them to tea on Sunday. Not a whole circus, just some jugglers and clowns and a baby elephant . . .

He remembered Mum was allergic to straw.

Then Keith's bedroom door creaked open and someone came into the room.

It was Dad.

Great, thought Keith, here am I trying to come up with ways to cheer them up, and Dad remembers another thing to be miserable about. What will it be this time? The pipe in the kitchen that bangs when you turn the hot tap off too quickly? Charlton's run of fourteen games away without a win? The government?

Dad sat down on the edge of the bed. In the darkness Keith could just make out his mouth.

Funny, thought Keith, it's not drooping.

'Son,' said Dad, and cleared his throat. 'Thanks for the birthday present. I've got to be honest and say I'd rather have had a pair of socks, but it's the thought that counts.'

Keith couldn't believe it.

Right up to bedtime Dad had been sighing and shaking his head and muttering about how it should be illegal to sell Tropical Mango Hi-Gloss to kids under eighteen.

What had happened?

Keith was still wondering when Dad leant forward and did something even more surprising.

He gave Keith a hug.

Keith hugged him back, heart thumping, trying to remember the last time they'd done this.

What had happened?

Then he remembered.

The cake.

When he'd given Dad his birthday cake earlier, Dad had just stared at it.

At first Keith had thought Dad didn't want it. Perhaps he didn't want to be reminded he was thirty-five. Perhaps he knew Keith had forgotten to wash his hands before making it. Perhaps he was allergic to iced chocolate sponge cake in the shape of a haddock.

Then Dad had given Keith a big slap on the back and said all sorts of stuff about what a great cake it was and how clever Keith was.

But he hadn't actually smiled.

Now Keith looked at Dad through the darkness.

'Did you really like the cake?' he asked.

He strained to see Dad's expression in the gloom.

Dad's lips moved.

Keith's heart leapt.

Was that a . . . ?

It was.

Dad was smiling.

'That,' said Dad, 'was a great cake.'

The smile slowly faded.

'Hope you didn't put too much sugar in. I'll be up all night burping if you did.'

Before Keith could say he'd only put six cups in, Dad squeezed his arm and was gone.

Keith lay there, heart thumping.

It was a start.

Keith had the idea later that night.

He slipped out of bed, crept into the hall and peeped into Mum and Dad's room.

All the lights were out.

He crept into the living-room, fumbled around in the sideboard drawer till he found the torch, then shone it into the bottom of the cupboard behind the TV.

There it was.

The slide projector.

He dragged it out, blew the dust off it and plugged it in. Then he piled the phone books onto the table, stood the projector on them and fiddled with the focus.

A big square of white light appeared on the wall.

Now, he thought, the slides.

He went back to the cupboard with the torch and rummaged around. An old brown vase toppled and fell. Keith caught it inches from the floor.

That's all I need, he thought. Dad storming out here with a rolled-up umbrella thinking we're being burgled.

He found the plastic boxes of slides and hunted through them for a box taken in the days when Mum and Dad still laughed.

An old one.

He found one marked 'Holidays'.

He knew that must be old, they hadn't had a holiday since he was about five.

Keith loaded the slides into the projector.

Click.

Him, huge on the wall, about three and a half, falling off a merry-go-round. That blur in the corner must be Dad, thought Keith.

Click.

Him, on a beach with a plastic bucket on his head.

Click.

Him, sitting on a donkey dripping ice-cream onto its neck.

Click. Click. Click.

Slides, swings, candy-floss.

All him.

The only sign of Mum or Dad was an occasional arm or a couple of legs.

Keith switched the torch back on and found an even older-looking slide box. He loaded the slides.

Click.

Mum and Dad, incredibly young, with longer hair and really bright jumpers, posing in front of a castle with serious expressions on their faces.

Serious expressions, Keith noticed, but no frown lines or droop lines.

Click.

Dad, the same age, posing with a platter of fish and chips. A red sash across his chest. Smiling.

Click.

Mum and Dad, sitting at a table in an outdoor restaurant on some sort of seaside pier. Arms round each other. Heads thrown back. Eyes sparkling.

Laughing.

Keith stared.

Then he noticed something else in the slide. The big flat fish on Mum and Dad's plates. And he remembered seeing the slide before, ages ago, when he was little. He'd asked Dad what the funny fish was called.

Dad had told him.

Dover sole.

'Dover sole,' said Keith now, out loud, as he looked at Mum and Dad's laughing faces.

They must really have liked Dover sole.

He looked at the slide for a few minutes more, then leant over to switch the projector off. He'd seen what he needed to see.

He bumped the slide box and it fell to the floor with a crash.

Keith looked anxiously towards Mum and Dad's room.

But it wasn't in Mum and Dad's room that the eruption of blankets took place.

It was on the settee.

Out of the darkness rose a crumpled figure, eyes screwed up, hair spiky, face twisted into a grimace.

Keith gasped. The blood pounded in his ears.

The figure's head was in the bright square of light on the wall.

Keith couldn't see who the head belonged to at first because Dad's laughing face was projected on top of it.

Then he saw who it was.

Dad.

He wasn't laughing.

* * *

Keith lay in bed and stared into the darkness.

He tried to think of pleasant things like how Dad, when he'd calmed down, had been quite reasonable about Keith looking at slides at one in the morning.

'Next time you can't sleep,' Dad had said, 'make do with a cup of hot milk, OK?'

Firm but fair, Keith had thought at the time. In between heart palpitations from the shock of Dad's appearance.

Now Keith's heart was beating fast for another reason.

Things were worse than he'd thought.

Mum and Dad didn't want to sleep together any more.

He had to move fast.

FOUR

Keith stood in a puddle of fishy water, waiting.

Come on Mr Gossage, he thought. Shake a leg.
Some of us have got to be at school in thirty-eight
minutes.

All around him the fish market was a confusion of
activity. Lorries and vans and piles of crates and
people shouting and blowing their horns. Everyone in
a hurry. Except Mr Gossage, who stood behind the
rippled glass of his office door like a frozen cod with a
phone to its ear.

Keith's hands were numb with the cold. He blew
on them and stuck them into his pockets and jingled
his life savings. £4.83. Two hundred and forty-one and
a half potatoes.

Wonder why Dover sole are so expensive, he
thought. Must be because they're so flat. Good for
sandwiches.

He hoped two hundred and forty-one and a half
potatoes would be enough.

The office door opened and Mr Gossage came out.

'OK, sunshine,' he boomed, 'what can I do for
you?'

'Two Dover sole please,' said Keith. 'Freshest

you've got.'

'Two boxes of sole coming up,' said Mr Gossage. 'Bit posh for your dad, isn't it?'

'Not two boxes,' said Keith, 'two fish.'

Mr Gossage looked at him.

'Sorry my old son, I'm a wholesaler. Can't split a box. Wholesalers don't split boxes or they wouldn't be wholesalers, would they? Try a fishmonger.'

He went back into the office.

'Our fishmonger doesn't have Dover sole,' shouted Keith.

'Try Selfridges,' shouted Mr Gossage, picking up the phone, 'or Dover.'

Keith walked gloomily away. Selfridges was half-way across London and mega-posh with it. Two hundred and forty-one and a half potatoes didn't get you a bag of chips up there. They wore diamond rings on their fish-fingers up there.

Oops, he thought, that's me nearly being a moaner. Think positive.

He thought positive. Perhaps he could get away with flattening a couple of mackerel between bricks.

Then he saw it.

It was propped up on top of a box of whitebait. At first Keith thought it was plastic, but as he got closer he saw it was real.

It was the colour of sunsets and tropical reefs and all of Aunty Joyce's lipsticks shimmering together. Each scale was a different colour and when Keith moved his head a fraction each scale was a different colour again.

It was the most beautiful fish he'd ever seen.

He imagined Mum and Dad seeing it. Their jaws dropping and their eyes widening as they opened the fridge and found themselves staring at a thousand shimmering pastel colours.

Forget Dover sole.

Forget mackerel with stretch-marks.

If this fish didn't cheer Mum and Dad up, nothing would.

Gripping his two hundred and forty-one and a half potatoes, Keith pushed through the circle of onlookers to ask how much.

'Twenty-five quid? For a fish?'

Dennis Baldwin looked at Keith as though he was a lunatic or a West Ham supporter or something. Then he went back to what he was doing.

CRASH.

Keith sighed.

It wasn't easy, trying to have a sensible conversation with someone who was more interested in smashing a supermarket trolley into a phone box.

'Five quid each,' said Keith. 'Take it in turns. You'll all get your money's worth.'

'Waste of time trying to cheer my mum and dad up,' said Eric Cox, as he started his run-up with the trolley. 'I've tried.'

CRASH.

Sally Prescott gripped the trolley. 'All mums and dads are depressed,' she said.

'No they're not,' said Keith.

'Course they are,' she said, taking aim. 'When was the last time you saw a mum or a dad having a really good time? Like they used to when they were kids.'

CRASH.

'Get your head examined,' said Rami Smith.

'Save your money,' said Mitch Wilson.

'I've got it,' said Dennis Baldwin. 'Buy your dad a fish-finger and paint it orange.'

CRASH.

Keith sighed.

Uncle Derek sighed.

'Look at that,' he said, handing Keith a small brown plastic box. 'Supposed to be British workmanship.'

Keith looked at the box.

'Hundreds of quid for a remote control garage door,' said Uncle Derek, 'and the remote control unit doesn't work.'

'I bet if you give it a prod with a screwdriver it'll work,' said Aunty Joyce.

'The screwdriver's in the garage,' said Uncle Derek through gritted teeth, 'and I can't get the garage door open.'

Keith wondered if Uncle Derek had forgotten what they were meant to be talking about.

'Bradley. Diana. Get you feet off the furniture,' snapped Uncle Derek.

Keith watched as his cousins took about half an hour to get their feet off the leather settee. He gave them a sympathetic shrug. They stuck their tongues out at him.

Tragic, thought Keith, only seven and nine, a bedroom each with fitted carpet, and they're like Uncle Derek already.

'So,' said Uncle Derek, 'what do you want to spend twenty-five quid on your dad for?'

'His birthday,' said Keith.

Uncle Derek stared at him.

'His birthday?'

Uncle Derek pulled a small black plastic box from his pocket, punched a few buttons and glared at the screen.

'Eighty-nine quid for a Computerized Pocket Organizer and it can't even remember a birthday. This country's going down the toilet.'

'It's Japanese,' said Aunty Joyce.

'They're just as bad,' said Uncle Derek.

Aunty Joyce picked up Uncle Derek's wallet.

'Don't worry about paying us back,' she said to Keith, 'just put our names on the card.'

Keith stood in the deserted market, shivering.

He wasn't sure if it was the cold or the excitement.

He watched the man wrap the fish in newspaper. The man handed him the bundle and he handed the man twenty-five pounds.

'By the way,' said the man, 'don't eat it, it's a bit old.'

Eat it, thought Keith as he hurried to the bus stop. Eat a fish that cost one thousand two hundred and fifty potatoes? Fat chance.

It was going in the freezer. Then, in the years to

come, whenever Mum and Dad were down in the dumps, he could get it out, give it a wipe, and watch the smiles spread across their faces.

He didn't put it in the freezer straight away.

He put it in the fridge because he wanted to surprise them. Sometimes they didn't open the freezer for days, but they opened the shop fridge about once every five minutes.

Five minutes passed.

They didn't open the fridge.

Keith hovered around the back of the shop watching Dad fillet some plaice and Mum mix up some batter.

He stared at the back of Dad's head and tried sending him an urgent telepathic message.

Open The Fridge.

Dad scratched his bottom.

Keith decided he'd better try something else.

He closed his eyes and made a wish.

I wish, he thought, that someone would walk into the shop now and ask Dad for something in the fridge.

It was worth a try. Even though none of the other forty-six thousand nine hundred and ninety-nine wishes he'd made in his life had come true.

The shop door opened and a man in a suit came in carrying a clipboard.

'Afternoon, sir, afternoon, madam,' said the man. 'Health inspection. Shall we start with the fridge?'

Keith grinned. Forty-seven thousandth time lucky.

Dad and Mum exchanged weary looks and Dad came over and opened the fridge.

Keith watched as Dad stopped and stared. The fish sat on the middle shelf, shimmering. Mum came over and she and Dad stood side by side, mouths slowly opening.

Keith didn't say anything. He waited for the amazed delight to creep over their faces.

The Health Inspector joined them. He bent down, head close to the fish.

He can't believe it's real, thought Keith.

The Health Inspector sniffed the fish.

Keith grinned. What did he think it was, plastic?

'How old's this fish?' asked the Health Inspector.

Keith stopped grinning. Everyone was looking at him. No one was looking amazed or delighted.

'Um, four or five days I think,' he said. 'It was flown in from abroad for a big hotel and they sent it back to the market cause it was the wrong sort. Perhaps a week.'

The Health Inspector sniffed the fish again.

Why's he doing that, wondered Keith. Does he think we're going to eat it?

Keith turned to Mum and Dad. 'Aren't the colours great?' he said. He had the awful thought that perhaps Mum and Dad were colour blind and had forgotten to tell him.

The Health Inspector straightened up.

'If the next time I look that fish isn't there,' he said slowly, 'I won't have to issue a summons for having stale fish on the premises, will I?'

No, thought Keith, you won't. Cause in a month's time when you're back it won't be there. It'll be in the freezer.

Then suddenly Keith had the fish in his hands. Dad had snatched it out of the fridge and thrust it at him.

Not now, thought Keith, wait till he's gone.

Dad put his face close to Keith's. It wasn't a happy face.

'Get it out of here,' he said, in a voice that was so quiet it sent a shiver down Keith's spine. 'Now.'

Keith opened his mouth to explain to the Health Inspector that it was all a misunderstanding and that the fish wasn't stale stock, it was more of a dead pet.

But Dad spoke again, and his voice was much louder.

'Take it outside and get rid of it. NOW.'

Keith stood in the drizzle, boiling.

OK, he thought, that's it. Enough. Finish.

If Mum and Dad want to be misery guts, they can be misery guts. But they aren't turning me into one.

He stared at the grey houses and the grey shops and the grey flats.

There must be somewhere in the world, he thought, where people are happy. Where Mums and Dads laugh, and sleep in the same bed, and paint their fish and chip shops orange without worrying about a few splashes on the pavement.

He looked down at the fish. The thousand pastel colours twinkled through the raindrops that covered it.

Bet you come from a place like that, he thought.

Then he heard a voice.

'Told you it wouldn't dry in this weather.'

Keith looked up.

Mr Naylor was standing in his doorway, prodding the paint on the front of the shop with his finger. He showed Keith his orange fingertip.

'You'll have to scrape it all off and start again.'

'Not me,' said Keith. 'I'm going abroad.'

FIVE

Mrs Lambert wasn't much help.

'Dunno,' she said, peering at the fish.

Come on, thought Keith, you're a geography teacher, you must have some idea where it comes from.

'Looks tropical,' said Mrs Lambert, struggling into her raincoat.

Keith sighed.

How could he plan his new life if he didn't know where his new life was going to be?

'Could be from the Caribbean,' said Mrs Lambert, buttoning up her coat. 'Though I'm guessing. I didn't get to eat any fish when I was there. Upset tummy.'

Keith's arms were hurting from holding the plastic bag open. He tried to jog her memory.

'Africa?'

Mrs Lambert looked at him quizzically.

'That's right. I had an upset tummy there too. How did you know?'

Keith sighed.

The travel agent wasn't much help either.

'Tropical,' he said, 'definitely tropical.'

He turned to his other customer, a woman in a dripping mac looking glumly through a pile of brochures.

'How about Greece again?' said the travel agent brightly.

The customer shook her head. 'The chips tasted of garlic.'

Great, thought Keith. Here am I trying to find out about my destiny and he's more worried about a week in Cairo or whatever the capital of Greece is.

'Spain?' said the travel agent. 'You liked Spain.'

The customer shook her head. 'Mum had her shopping trolley nicked.'

'Yugoslavia?'

'Palm trees were nylon.'

The customer peered into Keith's plastic bag at the fish.

'That's nice,' she said. 'I like that.'

She turned back to the travel agent.

'Where does that come from?' she asked.

'Greece,' said the travel agent, avoiding Keith's eyes.

Keith sighed.

The tropical fish expert at the Natural History Museum was a lot more help.

'Parrot fish,' he said. 'Found in the tropical north along the Great Barrier Reef.'

'Thanks,' said Keith.

'Anything else?' said the tropical fish expert.

'Yes,' said Keith. 'Where's the Great Barrier Reef?'

* * *

Keith stood looking up at the big old stone building. City traffic roared all around it. Pigeons perched high on its grimy window-sills.

For a moment he thought he'd come to the wrong place. Then he saw the sign.

Australia House.

When the man at the museum had told him about Australia House, Keith had imagined a blond brick bungalow with a barbeque and a swimming pool like in *Neighbours*.

Oh well, he thought, they probably couldn't get planning permission to build one like that in London.

He went in through the big doors.

The receptionist took a look inside the plastic bag and before Keith could ask her anything, she was talking into her phone.

'Carol,' she said, 'Come and have a look at this.'

A woman with hair just like a couple of the women in *Neighbours* came out of a side door and looked into the bag.

'Don't see many of those here in Pommyland,' she said.

Keith explained about the hotel and the market and the museum.

'This Great Barrier Reef,' he said finally, 'is it anywhere near Ramsay Street?'

The receptionist and the woman grinned at each other.

Nice, thought Keith. Instead of grinning like a couple of loonies, how about lending me an Australian street directory?

'Come in here,' said the woman.

She led Keith into an office. On the wall was a map of Australia. The woman pointed to a place called Melbourne right down the bottom.

'Ramsay Street, legend has it, is here,' she said. 'The Great Barrier Reef is up here.' She ran her finger along the coastline at the top right hand corner of Australia.

'Is it a happy sort of place?' asked Keith.

The woman grinned again. 'It's underwater,' she said, 'but apart from that it's pretty happy.'

She pointed to a poster further along the wall.

'Here's your bloke here.'

Along the top of the poster it said 'Fish Of The Great Barrier Reef'. The woman was pointing to a fish just like the one in Keith's bag.

Keith stared.

There were hundreds of them. Hundreds of multi-coloured fish. All different. All with different names. He imagined Mum and Dad's faces, seeing this. Then he remembered he wasn't trying to cheer them up anymore.

'Beautiful, aren't they?' said the woman. 'Beaches up that way aren't too bad, either.'

She pointed to another poster behind Keith.

He turned round.

It was like a dream, except that Keith's dreams were mostly like the telly with the colour turned up too high.

This was perfect.

A deserted beach of white sand with palm trees

hanging over it and a turquoise sea lapping at the edge. And the bluest sky he'd ever seen.

The only sign of human habitation was a wooden sign on a post in the shade of one of the palm trees.

Keith couldn't read what the sign said, but he knew anyway.

No Misery Guts.

He realised he'd been gazing at the poster for ages and the woman was looking at him.

Never mind. She'd understand when he explained to her that he'd just found the place where he was going to spend the rest of his life.

All the way home on the train Keith saw nothing but the beach.

Waterloo Bridge, the Bermondsey Gas Works, the Deptford tower blocks and several thousand gallons of dirty rain slid past the carriage window and Keith missed them all.

He was working out how long till he could get away.

Dennis Baldwin's older brother had left home when he was fourteen. Though that had been to go to a juvenile correction centre.

The train pulled into Keith's station and he realised with a shock where he was.

He opened the plastic bag and looked at the fish.

'Thanks,' he said.

Then he left the fish on the seat so that someone else could find it and have their life changed as well.

* * *

Mum was writing something at the kitchen table when he got in.

She looked up.

'Keith,' she said, 'here a minute.'

Keith's stomach sank. School must have rung up about him being away for the afternoon.

'Love,' she said, 'about the other night. Dad and me hadn't had a fight. He was on the settee because his tummy was playing up and he kept fidgeting and keeping me awake.'

Despite the fact that he wasn't meant to be giving a toss about Dad any more, Keith felt a twinge of concern.

'Not an ulcer?' he said.

'No,' said Mum. 'Your cake.'

Keith wasn't sure whether to feel relieved or offended.

'Well, partly your cake,' Mum continued. 'He hasn't been sleeping well for a few months.'

She sighed and Keith tried to count the frown lines on her forehead. He got lost at eleven.

'Things are getting him down,' she said.

Another entry, thought Keith, for The Most Incredibly Obvious Statement Ever Made.

'What have you got there?' asked Mum.

Keith realised the bundle of Australia House brochures he'd been holding under his jacket had slipped and a couple had fallen onto the floor.

Mum picked one up. She looked at it. Escape To Queensland's Tropical Far North, it said.

'Are you doing a project on Australia at school?'

Keith was about to say yes, then stopped himself. This was his new life. He didn't want to lie about it.

He didn't say anything.

Mum was looking at the brochure wistfully.

'Looks like paradise,' she said. 'That's what we could do with, a bit of that.'

Keith realised his heart was beating fast.

Mum handed him the brochure.

'Dreams,' she said, mostly to herself. She went back to her writing.

Later, in his room, a thought came to him. That was the first time he'd ever seen Mum doing the pools.

Keith crouched on the stairs and watched Dad at the fryers, skimming golden lumps of cod and rock salmon out of the foaming oil and sliding them into the heated cabinet.

He'd always liked watching Dad fry. Dad looked good over the fryers, even when he was a bit grumpy. The cabinet lights made his face shine and the steam made his hair curl at the front.

Tonight, though, Keith wasn't looking at the shining cheeks or the curly hair. He was looking at the droopy mouth lines and the dark patches under Dad's eyes.

I can't do it, he thought.

I can't leave them here to plod through a life of sleepless nights and cheap flour and freezing rain and Owen the milkman.

Every time I lie back on that white sand and take a sip from a coconut and let the warm sea breezes clear up a pimple, I'll be thinking of them back here, being misery guts.

Dad lowered a basket of chips into the fryer and the oil bubbled noisily. He stood watching it, shoulders stooped.

I'll have to take them with me, thought Keith.

The thought made something bubble up inside him. Fear, excitement, indigestion, he wasn't sure.

'Dad,' he said as casually as he could, strolling into the shop.

Dad looked up.

'Have you ever thought of . . . um . . . moving?'

'Where?' said Dad.

'Um . . . down south. Quite a long way down south.'

'What,' said Dad, 'Lewisham?' He thought about it and shrugged. 'No point.'

'Further south than that,' said Keith. 'Australia.'

Dad looked at him, taken aback.

'Australia?'

Keith nodded.

Dad suddenly swung round and started frantically scooping pieces of plaice out of the oil. Keith saw they were a bit burnt.

Dad turned back to him, mouth almost drooping to the floor.

'I can't even cook fish properly here any more. Why would I want to go to Australia?'

SIX

Keith pressed the button on the slide projector.

Click.

Grandpa appeared on the wall, asleep in a deck-chair on a pebble beach under a grey sky.

'Didn't rain the whole week we were away,' said Nan to Mum, who was sitting next to her on the settee.

Keith shone his torch onto the projector. Only four slides left.

I'll have to do it soon, he thought. His tummy gave a quiver.

'It was windy, mind,' Nan continued, 'but it didn't rain once.'

'Yes it did,' growled Grandpa. 'Rained the Thursday night. Twice.'

'No it didn't,' said Nan. 'That was wind.'

Keith heard Dad give a long sort of sigh from the back of the room.

Nan turned to Mum again. 'You lot should think about getting away, Marge. You haven't been away for years.'

'I know we haven't,' said Mum wearily. 'Trouble is, holidays aren't easy, what with the shop and everything. Still . . .'

'Next slide, Keith,' said Dad.

Keith took a deep breath.

OK, he thought, this is it. Ten nine eight seven six five four three two one.

Click.

On the wall appeared a gleaming stretch of white sand. An expanse of sparkling turquoise sea. Palm trees against a clear blue sky.

Nice one, thought Keith. Worth every penny of the return trip to Australia House and the ninety potatoes for the slide.

'Blimey,' said Nan. 'That's not Worthing.'

'Bognor,' said Grandpa. 'That's Bognor, that is.'

'Chemist must have mixed them up,' said Nan. She peered at the screen. 'Doesn't look like Bognor.'

Keith fumbled in the dark for his cassette player. He pressed the play button. The sound of a gentle surf filled the room.

At least that's what Keith hoped the others would think it was. Rather than the sound of an RV 106 steam locomotive climbing a hill just outside Swansea which had been the closest thing to a gentle surf on Rami Smith's dad's sound effects record.

'What's that noise?' said Grandpa. 'Is there a gas leak?'

'Keith,' said Mum, 'what's going on?'

Keith switched on the torch and shone it on the brochure in his other hand. He started reading in a loud and what he hoped was persuasive voice.

'Tropical Australia, idyllic paradise where your

troubles and cares are as far away as yesterday . . .'

'Keith,' said Dad. He didn't sound as though his troubles and cares were as far away as yesterday.

Keith pressed on. '. . . where warm, fragrant breezes murmur songs of happiness . . .'

He pulled a can of air-freshener from his pocket and sprayed some in the general direction of the others.

'. . . and where rainbow choirs of exotic birds proclaim the joys tomorrow holds in store.'

He put down the torch, the brochure and the air-freshener, cupped his hands to his mouth and made what he hoped was the happy sound of an exotic tropical bird. Mr Smith's record had only had ducks.

In the darkness Keith could just make out Mum and Dad and Nan and Grandad staring at him, open-mouthed.

It's working, he thought, they're stunned by the beauty of the place.

He saw they were all frowning.

They're thinking, he told himself, thinking why didn't they go there years ago.

Dad snapped the light on.

'Keith,' he said quietly, 'I said I didn't want to hear another thing about Australia.'

'Australia?' said Nan.

'It's all right, Mum,' said Mum.

Keith decided to swing his emergency plan into operation. He thrust his hand down behind the arm-chair cushion and pulled out the soft pink and gold fruit that had cost him a hundred and sixty potatoes at Selfridges.

He put it on the coffee table in front of them all.

'The mango,' he said, 'is just part of nature's bounty in Australia's tropical wonderland . . .'

'Keith . . .' said Dad.

'Keith . . .' said Mum.

'We'll be able to have fresh ones for breakfast every day,' said Keith.

Nan gripped Mum's arm in alarm. 'Marge, what's all this about Australia? You're not . . .?'

'Australia?' said Grandad. 'Nobody said anything to me about Australia.'

'There's no way you'd get us going to a place like that,' said Nan. 'Mrs Bridge's daughter went. They don't even have corned beef in tins.'

'Mum . . .' said Mum.

'Typical,' said Grandad, 'nobody ever tells me anything.'

'There's nothing to tell,' said Dad.

'Mangoes grow on trees out there,' said Keith. 'They just fall onto the streets. Knee-deep sometimes . . .'

'KEITH,' roared Dad, 'BE QUIET.'

The whole room went quiet.

'We are not,' said Dad, almost whispering, 'going to Australia.'

Keith lay in bed with his eyes closed, trying to remember.

It was his favourite memory, the one of him when he was a little kid, three or something. He was in a park, watching an ant with wings climb up a dande-

lion. Next to him on the grass Mum and Dad were talking and laughing softly to each other. Then they went quiet. He looked up at them. They were both gazing at him, smiling gently, eyes shining.

Keith squeezed his eyes shut tighter, trying to see the memory more clearly.

Lately, each time he'd tried, the memory had been getting blurrier and blurrier.

Now, as Keith pushed his fists into his eyelids, he couldn't even see the kid's face.

Perhaps it wasn't even him.

Keith dusted the pieces of mango with flour and slid them through the bowl of creamy batter and dropped them into the bubbling fat.

Then he opened a tin and did the same with some pineapple rings.

When they'd all turned golden brown be scooped them out with the spatula and put them onto a plate.

He blew hard onto a piece of mango for a couple of minutes, then put it into his mouth.

Mmm. Nice one. A bit fishy, but otherwise delicious.

He heard footsteps on the stairs and Mum came into the shop.

'I thought I could smell frying,' she said sleepily. 'Keith, what are you doing? It's Sunday.'

'Making breakfast,' said Keith. 'A typical Australian breakfast.'

Mum's shoulders sagged. Then she stared at Keith. 'What have you done to your shirt?'

'It's tropical,' said Keith.

Mum closed her eyes.

All right, thought Keith, it's not the most perfect tropical shirt in London but it's not bad for a first effort.

Next time he'd have to use a tape measure when he cut the sleeves short so they ended up the same length. And he'd have to learn to paint tropical birds a bit better too.

Mum opened her eyes.

'Why's it got socks on it?'

'They're parrots.'

Mum took a deep breath.

'Don't let Dad see it, Keith. After last night he's liable to do something drastic.'

'I just want us all to be happy,' said Keith. 'We'd be happy in Australia, I know we would.'

Mum looked at him for a long time.

Finally she spoke. 'I want us to be happy too, love, and I'd go to Timbuctoo if I thought it'd make any difference.'

She looked around the empty shop and out into the overcast street.

'But this is our life and we've just got to make the best of it. Now get that shirt off before Dad gets up.'

'What shirt?' said Dad, coming into the shop in his dressing-gown.

He stopped and stared at Keith's shirt.

Keith saw his forehead clench into angry ripples. Even more than Mum could get on hers.

Dad opened his mouth to speak.

Keith opened his mouth to speak.

Mum beat them both to it.

'I know,' she said, 'let's have a day at the seaside. We haven't been to the seaside for years. Let's have a day at Worthing.'

Keith sat on a deckchair, freezing.

He looked at Mum, sitting on her deckchair, coat buttoned up and scarf wrapped round her throat, doing some knitting. He could tell she was purposely not looking at him.

He looked at Dad, sitting in his deckchair, coat buttoned up, reading the paper. Dad was purposely not looking at him too.

Keith shivered and wished he'd left the sleeves on his tropical shirt. He pulled his jacket tighter round him and wondered if the numbness in his arms was nervous tension or frost-bite.

He looked at Mum again.

She smiled at him. He knew it wasn't a real smile. It was the half-hearted lip-stretch people do on windy beaches on overcast days when they want to pretend they're having fun.

Keith looked out across the pebbles. This is ridiculous, he thought. Two hours we've been here and neither of them have asked me why I've got a white nose.

He touched his nose to make sure the white coating was still on it.

Yep.

Ask me, thought Keith, ask me.

Because then he could tell them.

'It's the zinc cream people wear in Australia to protect their noses from the sun that shines all day, every day, 365 days of the year.'

And then they'd have to ask themselves why they were freezing to death on Worthing beach when they could be lying under palm trees in North Queensland.

Keith hoped they couldn't tell it was really toothpaste.

He sent a double-strength telepathic message to Mum.

Ask me.

Mum closed her eyes and looked as though she was dropping off to sleep.

Keith sighed and decided to get the 50p back he'd paid Dennis Baldwin to teach him the secret of telepathy. Then Dad suddenly screwed up his newspaper and jumped to his feet.

Blimey, thought Keith, my aim must have been crooked.

But Dad didn't mention white noses or white sandy beaches.

'OK, that's it,' he shouted into the wind. 'Enough. Finish. We're going home.'

He started stuffing the thermos and blankets into the picnic bag. Mum opened her eyes, went to say something, then changed her mind.

'We can't go yet,' said Keith. 'I've only just put my zinc cream on.'

Dad came over to Keith and grabbed him by the arm. It hurt.

At least I haven't got frost-bite, thought Keith.

'I'm only going to say this once more,' said Dad, 'so listen very carefully. We are not ever, under any circumstances, going to Australia.'

Nobody spoke on the drive back to London.

Keith sat in the back of the van and stared out into the dusk and tried not to feel sad about going to Australia by himself and leaving Mum and Dad behind and probably never seeing them again.

Why should I feel sad, he thought.

It's their fault.

I tried.

He felt his eyes getting hot and prickly.

See, he thought, it's happening already. I'm turning into a misery guts.

He took his mind off things by working out how many potatoes it would take for him to save up the plane fare.

Twenty-five thousand.

He'd better start tomorrow.

Then he closed his eyes and thought about warm white sand and warm turquoise lagoons and glorious pink tropical sunsets.

He opened his eyes just as the van was turning into his street and for a moment he thought he could see one.

A glorious pink tropical sunset.

Then he realised what it was.

A fire.

Blimey, he thought, one of the buildings in our

street's on fire.

Suddenly the van was surrounded by red flashing lights and screaming sirens and men running with hoses.

'Whose place is it?' said Mum.

'Can't see,' said Dad.

The van moved slowly forward and Keith tried to see whose place it was.

Then he remembered.

The fryer.

The one he'd cooked breakfast in.

He'd forgotten to switch it off.

SEVEN

Keith stood in his street at dawn looking at the sooty wall with the black holes that used to be his life.

The black hole that used to be the kitchen.

The black hole that used to be his bedroom.

The black hole that used to be the shop.

He looked at the edges of the shop hole to see if there was a tiny bit of Tropical Mango that might cheer him up a bit.

Nothing.

Just charred wood and a yellow plastic strip that the fireman had tied across the shop to stop people going in and pinching stuff.

Not that there was anything left to pinch.

Keith realised Mitch Wilson was standing next to him with a bikeload of newspapers, staring at the black holes. After a bit Mitch pulled their paper from his bag, folded it up, handed it to Dad and hurried off, his bike wheels crunching over the glass that used to be the shop window.

Mum started sobbing and Dad put his arm round her.

Owen's milk float pulled up with a whine. Owen stared at the black holes.

'What happened?' he asked.

Nobody answered.

Keith realised he was the one who should speak.

'I burnt it down,' he said.

So this is what it feels like to be a misery guts, thought Keith.

He had a vision of spending the rest of his life doing what he'd been doing for most of the day. Lying on cousin Bradley's bed in Aunty Joyce's old bathrobe feeling like there was a black hole inside him bigger than any of the ones he'd seen that morning.

The intergalactic gladiators on the posters around Bradley's bedroom wall glared down at him. Keith knew what they were thinking.

Misery guts.

He stood up.

OK, he thought. The only way I'm going to get out of turning into a misery guts is to think positive.

He picked up all his clothes and laid them out carefully on the bed.

Jacket, scarf, tropical shirt, vest, jeans, socks, underpants, shoes.

He emptied out the pockets of his jacket and jeans and laid those things out too.

Penknife, 84p, hanky, potato peeler, slide of tropical beach, school bus pass, half a stick of Worthing rock, tube of toothpaste.

Could be worse, he thought. Plenty of kids in the world haven't even got this much. Plenty of kids in the world, if they lost everything in a fire it'd be a pair of shorts, a T-shirt and a plastic bowl, not a desk with two drawers and a cassette player with detachable speakers and a collection of Green Shield stamps that only needed another 8940 books for the Ford Escort and a leather football and a book about mountain climbers and a life membership to the Ronnie Barker fan club and a . . .

Stop it.

Think positive.

Mum and Dad still had the clothes they were wearing and there was the van and the picnic basket and the thermos and the deckchairs.

What more did they need to drive to Australia?

He could hear Dad and Uncle Derek downstairs talking to the man from the insurance. Surely the insurance money would be enough to pay for the ferry rides over the sea bits.

I've got a choice, thought Keith.

I can go downstairs and tell Mum and Dad how sorry I am and we can all sit around being miserable.

Or I can go down and make it up to them by persuading them to come to Australia where they'll be happy for ever and ever.

It wasn't even a choice really.

'Insurance,' Uncle Derek was saying, shaking his head, 'you pay through the nose, then when it's their turn it's a different story.'

The leather armchair Dad was sitting in groaned.

Keith was shocked by how droopy Dad's mouth

was. Have to go carefully in Australia, he thought. Too much grinning too quickly and Dad could strain something.

'They're being fair,' Dad was saying, 'none of the shop equipment was new, or our furniture and clothes and stuff, so you can't expect them to pay the cost of buying new stuff.'

The room fell silent.

None of them had seen Keith standing in the doorway. He hitched up his bathrobe.

This was his chance.

He ran through in his head the speech he'd prepared about how it didn't matter so much about being poor if you were happy.

He was about to start saying it when he noticed Mum's eyes. The rims were bright red. She must have been crying for hours.

Suddenly the words Keith had planned to say were scrambled up in his head.

'Will you have enough to open a new shop?' asked Aunty Joyce as she sat down on the settee next to Mum.

The settee groaned.

'Don't know,' said Dad.

Keith stopped trying to remember his first speech and rehearsed the second one, the one about how it was cheaper to open up fish and chip shops near tropical beaches because you didn't have to spend anything on heating and you could get free salt off the rocks.

He was about to start saying it when Dad sighed.

It was the saddest sigh Keith had ever heard.

He had a vision of them all turning to him after he'd said his speech and just looking at him with long faces and Dad doing another one of those sighs.

He didn't speak.

Uncle Derek sat back in his chair and crossed his legs. The chair groaned.

'Come and work for me,' he said to Dad. 'Roof insulation's a growth industry. Big opportunities. OK, you'll have to hoof it round the country with a salesman's bag at first, but after a few years, who knows? I'm thinking of expanding into remote control garage doors.' His face fell. 'That's if I can find one that actually works.'

'Thanks, Derek,' said Dad in a flat voice. 'I'll er . . . I'll think about it.'

Keith frantically tried to remember his final speech, the one about the 937 varieties of tropical fish on the Great Barrier Reef.

'You can stay with us as long as you like,' said Aunty Joyce, 'we've got the spare room and Bradley doesn't mind sharing with Keith.'

Bradley, hunched in front of the TV, turned and glared at Keith.

Is it 937, thought Keith desperately, or 973?

'Thanks, Joyce,' said Mum, 'but we couldn't.'

'Don't worry about the financial side,' said Aunty Joyce, 'you can make it up to us in babysitting. You'd like that, wouldn't you, Diana?'

Diana, lying on the floor picking the plastic veneer off her walkman, looked up at Mum.

'Our last babysitter,' she said, 'cut her head open on the microwave.'

Nearly a thousand, thought Keith, that'll do.

He opened his mouth to speak.

But Mum and Dad, sitting there, looked so unhappy that Keith couldn't get the words out.

When people were that unhappy it just seemed wrong to try and cheer them up.

Keith had never felt that before in his life but he did now.

And with an awful feeling of dread, he realised what it meant.

It's happened, he thought. I've become a misery guts.

In bed that night he tried everything he could think of to cheer himself up.

Jokes, Ronnie Barker sketches he knew off by heart, a replay of the time the school team beat Kidbrooke six-nil, memories of when Eric Cox's mum worked in a chocolate frog factory and she was allowed to bring home the ones without legs.

No good.

He was a misery guts.

As he finally drifted off to sleep, he was half aware of Mum and Dad coming into the room.

They must be sick of all the roof insulation stacked in the spare room, he thought sleepily, and rolled over in bed to make space for them.

'Keith,' said Dad, 'are you awake?'

Keith struggled awake.

Bradley was snoring on the blow-up bed on the floor.

Mum and Dad led Keith to the spare room. They sat him on the bed and stood over him. Keith could see piles of roof insulation looming up behind them.

'Fourteen years we kept that shop going,' said Dad, 'and now it's finished.'

Here it comes, thought Keith sadly. The accusations. The blame.

'I'm sorry, Dad,' he said.

'Half a million pieces of fish we sold,' said Dad.

'I'm sorry.'

'Twenty-five million chips. Two hundred thousand pickled onions. A hundred thousand bags of peas. And now I'm faced with spending the rest of my life selling roof insulation.'

'Dad,' said Keith miserably, 'I'm sorry. I forgot about the fryer. It's my fault.'

'Keith,' said Mum, 'Dad and I have made a decision.'

Here it comes, thought Keith. The punishment.

What would it be? Making him leave school to get a job to pay them back? A juvenile correction centre?

'We've decided,' said Dad, 'to go to Australia.'

EIGHT

On the plane to Istanbul, Keith wrote a postcard.

Dear Uncle Derek and Aunty Joyce,

Please thank your friend the travel agent for fixing up the cheap tickets. When Dad found out how much the full-price ones were I thought he was going to change his mind. I could tell from your faces you thought he was too. Love to Bradley and Diana and Mum hopes Bradley's rash from the blow-up bed has cleared up.

Love, Keith.

At Istanbul Airport he wrote another.

Dear Nan and Grandad,

Thanks for the tropical shirt. I'm saving it to wear when we land in Australia. I'll also wear it when we've got rich and you come out for a visit. Nan, I've checked up and you can't get cholera or typhoid in Australia, or Yangtze Fever, so don't worry. Mum and Dad are well, but Dad is in a bit of a bad mood. He says seven and a half hours is too long to wait between planes. I think he just can't wait to get to Australia.

Love, Keith.

He wrote two more on the plane to Karachi.

Dear Mr Naylor,

Mum asked me to drop you a line to say thanks for having us to tea last Tuesday and she's very glad the fire didn't damage your wallpaper. It's a small world. Dad is sitting next to a German salesman who sells wallpaper. He's been telling Dad all about it for over three hours.

Your ex-neighbour, Keith Shipley.

PS. Thankfully you were wrong about taking off in planes. We've done it twice now and none of our eardrums have exploded.

Dear Owen,
Please cancel all milk deliveries to our place, if you haven't already.
Yours sincerely, Keith Shipley.

And another two at Karachi Airport.

Dear Mrs Lambert,
Guess what? We're in Pakistan and we've got upset tummies too. I reckon it's the sandwiches we bought when they said our next flight was delayed ten hours. Was the plane delayed on your trip to Africa? Please tell the class they're very welcome to visit us in Australia at any time and that goes for you too but I'd stick to biscuits at the airports.
Yours faithfully, Keith Shipley, Indian subcontinent.

Dear Mr Crouch,
I've just been talking to a cleaner who used to live in Bristol till he was deported and he says they're short of good science teachers here in Pakistan. Bear in mind that the language might be a problem. Dad spent ten minutes trying to tell the guard at the security gate he was only going to Australia cause

Mum wanted to. The guard thought he was talking about radial tyres.

Your ex-student, K. Shipley.

PS. I'm sure Dad was only joking.

On the plane to Colombo he wrote another.

Dear Dennis,

My parents have stopped talking to each other just like yours did on holiday in Dorset. They haven't hit each other with any chairs yet though. This is because they know Australia will be wonderful once we get there. Tell Sally Prescott that in Australia all mums and dads are happy.

Keith.

And another on the plane to Jakarta.

Dear Rami,

All the airports we've been to on this trip have had armed soldiers guarding them. I think this is to stop all the local people crowding onto the planes to get to Australia. Sorry I didn't hang around the other day but it's very hard saying goodbye to people who are in the middle of kicking the seats out of a bus shelter.

Keith.

He wrote the last one on the plane to Cairns.

Dear Uncle Derek and Aunty Joyce,

Please tell your friend the travel agent that five different airlines is a bit too much for older people. I'm fine, but 73 hours is a long trip when you're over 30. I'm sure Mum and Dad would send their love if they were awake.

Love, Keith.

Then the pilot announced that they had just commenced flying over the continent of Australia.

Keith forgot his stomach, which felt like a knotted hosepipe. He forgot his mouth, which felt like a bath that hadn't been wiped out for months. He forgot his eyes, which felt like tinned peaches in bowls of cornflakes.

Australia.

He peered out of the window.

Far below he could see browns and greens and the flash of sun on water.

He turned to Mum and Dad, to shake them and hug them and let them see for themselves. But their sleeping faces looked so exhausted he decided not to wake them up.

Plenty of time for grinning and hugging each other when they were on the ground.

At Orchid Cove.

For about the ten thousandth time since the woman at Australia House had told him what the tropical beach on her wall was called, Keith said the words quietly to himself.

Orchid Cove.

He had a sudden urge to do some cartwheels up the aisle of the plane.

Instead he went into one of the plane toilets and changed into Nan and Grandad's tropical shirt. It was green and purple with scenes of tourist attractions in Hawaii on it.

Who cares, thought Keith happily. It's tropical. He smeared some toothpaste on his nose.

As he walked back to his seat he noticed that for the first time some of the other passengers were smiling.

He smiled back.

Australia, he thought. What other country could cheer up a planeload of misery guts at sixty thousand feet?

Keith didn't notice the heat until they were on the airport bus into Cairns.

He was staring out the window, marvelling at how bright the shops and houses were even though he was wearing the sunglasses he'd bought in Lewisham.

'I think,' said Dad, 'we should try and find a shop here in Cairns.'

Keith's stomach gave a lurch. Cairns looked like a nice place, much cleaner and brighter than London, but he'd only counted four palm trees since they'd left the airport and the only stretch of sand he'd seen was in a builder's yard. And Orchid Cove was only one more bus ride away.

'Dad,' he said desperately, 'look at all the fish and chip shops and hamburger places and pizza parlours and take-away Chinese restaurants.'

As he spoke he prayed they'd pass some. They did, a row of shops with at least one of each.

'Keith's right, love,' said Mum. 'Let's go and have a look at Orchid Cove.'

The bus turned a corner and they passed another fish and chip shop.

'All right,' said Dad.

Keith's pulse slowed down. He realised he was dripping with sweat.

And the bus was air-conditioned.

The bus to Orchid Cove wasn't air-conditioned.

Keith decided it was like sitting in a warm bath that was over your head but you could still breathe.

He liked it.

But it did make you feel very sleepy.

He watched the suburbs of Cairns slipping past the window, then fields of green stuff that were higher than the bus. Giant shallots, he thought sleepily.

He had a vision of an Australian salad. Lettuce leaves as big as bedspreads. Tomatoes as big as bubble-cars. Cucumbers as big as tube trains.

Then someone was shaking his shoulder.

Keith opened his eyes.

It was Mum.

The light outside the bus had changed. It wasn't bright anymore, it was dull, but glowing at the same time.

Keith staggered off the bus behind Mum and Dad. The bus driver dragged their suitcases out of the luggage compartment, climbed back in, and the bus roared away down the narrow road.

Keith saw why the light was different. The sky was glowing with pink and gold and purple and a colour that made his tired eyes open wide.

Tropical Mango.

Across the road, tall and dark against the sunset, a row of slender trunks hung over a sandy beach, fronds gently swaying.

Palm trees.

Keith walked slowly over and stood under the palm trees on the warm sand and watched the waves breaking, pink and frothy like the strawberry milkshake he'd had a couple of hours earlier.

A warm breeze blew against his face. He took a deep breath and smelled more wonderful tropical smells than he'd ever smelled before. Even including the time Bradley dropped the iron onto Aunty Joyce's bottles of perfume.

Keith felt two arms slide around his shoulders. He looked up. Mum and Dad were standing close to him, their faces aglow with huge smiles.

Paradise.

NINE

Keith opened his eyes and didn't know where he was.

Above his head was a curved metal ceiling with rivets in it.

Then he remembered.

Van Number Six, Orchid Cove Caravan Park, Orchid Cove, Paradise.

Over in the other bed Mum and Dad were still asleep. Keith looked at his watch. Six-thirty Australian time. He pulled the curtain aside. Sunlight spilled onto his bed.

Fantastic, he thought.

He lay back for a bit and just enjoyed having sunlight on his bed at six-thirty in the morning. Then he got down to business.

OK. Plan for the day. Explore paradise, then when Mum and Dad wake up, take them on the grand tour.

Nice one.

He slipped out of bed and put on his tropical shirt and his new shorts, the ones Mum had made him on Aunty Joyce's Swedish sewing-machine. He put his shoes on with no socks. Then he put some toothpaste on his nose and stepped quietly out of the caravan.

The air was clean and warm and smelt like air-freshener only much better.

In the lush green forest at the back of the caravan park Keith could see flashes of colour as red and blue birds swooped among the trees. They looked like West Ham practising diving headers.

He walked down to the beach. It was even better than the night before.

In the morning sun the sand was a brilliant white and the sea was a sparkling turquoise. The sky was deep blue and the fronds of the palm trees shone emerald green.

Perfect, thought Keith. Just like the poster in Australia House.

Except for the girl fishing.

He stood and watched as the girl down near the water's edge swung her big rod and cast her line out over the waves.

I wonder if fishing's easy to learn, he thought. Be handy, me popping down here before breakfast each morning and catching all the fish for the shop.

She didn't look any older than him.

He went closer for a better look, down onto the wet sand where the girl was standing.

She turned and stared at him. Her eyes were almost as pale as her hair and her face was very brown.

Keith noticed pink patches where the brown was peeling off her nose and wondered if he should offer her some toothpaste.

He decided not to.

'Hello, I'm Keith.'

'G'day, I'm Tracy.'

'Caught anything?'

'Bit of a cough last winter. Better now but.'

She grinned at him.

Keith grinned back. Here they were, only met two seconds ago and she was cracking jokes already. What a place.

The water looked cool and tempting. Keith kicked off his shoes and stepped in up to his ankles.

'Wouldn't if I was you,' said Tracy.

'Why not?' said Keith.

'Stingers.'

Keith looked at her blankly.

Stingers?

'Sea Wasps,' said Tracy.

Sea Wasps?

Keith knew all about wasps, he'd had plenty attack his jam sandwiches on picnics, and he knew they couldn't live underwater, because he and Dennis Baldwin had tried to teach one to swim once. Must be another joke.

'Box jellyfish,' said Tracy slowly and more loudly. She held out a pair of green tights to Keith. 'Put these on if you want to go for a paddle. Won't stop them stinging you but at least the mongrels won't kill you.'

Kill?

Keith stepped quickly out of the water.

Tracy pointed towards the palm trees. 'It's got all about 'em over there.'

Keith saw Tracy was pointing to a sign on a wooden pole.

Keith recognised it as the sign he hadn't been able

to read in the Australia House poster.

He walked into the shade of the palm trees and read the sign. Blimey, he thought, she's right. Box jellyfish. Waters around North Queensland coast. Sting fatal.

Keith felt panic starting in his stomach.

Killer jellyfish?

In paradise?

What would Mum and Dad say when they found out he'd brought them twelve thousand miles on five different airlines to a place with killer jellyfish?

He forced himself to calm down.

OK, so they wouldn't be able to swim in the sea. No big deal. They could still lie on the white sand under the swaying palm fronds.

He looked up at the palm tree he was standing under. Around the base of the fronds, high above him, he saw a cluster of big round greeny-brown things. It took him a moment to work out what they were.

Coconuts.

Suddenly he felt fine again. What were a few killer jellyfish compared to being able to lie back in the shade, drinking from a fresh coconut?

'Wouldn't stay under there too long,' yelled Tracy.

Why not? thought Keith.

'Split your skull open if one of 'em falls on you.'

Keith looked at the palm tree. It must be a hundred years old, how was it going to fall on him? Then he realised Tracy meant the coconuts.

Keith looked down the beach at her and wondered if she was only nine and big for her age. Nine year olds panicked about things like coconuts falling on you.

Tracy was yelling at him again, pointing across the road.

'Look over there.'

Keith turned and looked.

Across the road was a high fence and behind it Keith could see the top of what looked like a hotel. Just inside the fence was another row of palm trees. Two men up ladders were cutting the coconuts off and throwing them down.

Must be the coconut harvest, thought Keith.

'Go and ask them what they're doing,' yelled Tracy.

Keith went over, feeling a bit of a wally, but curious.

'What are you doing?' he called up.

'We're missile experts,' said one of the men with a grin, 'removing dangerous missiles. Bit of a breeze and these mongrels'd drop on your head and crack your skull open.'

As he spoke he accidently knocked one of the coconuts with his arm. It hurtled down and smacked into the road near Keith.

The man looked down, alarmed. 'Jeez, sorry,' he said. 'You'd better shift away a bit.'

Keith looked at the coconut at his feet. It wasn't even cracked. Then he saw the dent in the tarmac where the coconut had hit the road.

Killer coconuts and killer jellyfish.

Keith had a sudden urge to run back to the caravan, crawl back into bed and pretend none of this had happened.

Instead he walked back down the beach to Tracy, who he decided was definitely the same age as him.

'Heard one drop,' said Tracy, 'thought you'd copped it for a sec.'

'Tracy,' said Keith, 'is there any other dangerous stuff round here?'

Tracy squinted out to sea.

'Not really,' she said.

Keith felt relief seep through him.

'There's the stonefish of course,' said Tracy, 'but they only kill you if you tread on them. Little mongrels lie on the bottom looking like rocks.'

Keith looked down to see if he was standing on any rocks.

'And the pufferfish,' continued Tracy, 'but you've got to actually eat a bit of one before you die.'

Think positive, thought Keith.

'What about rivers? Are there any good rivers for swimming in?'

'Some beauties,' said Tracy. 'The crocs come from miles around to swim in 'em.'

Crocs, thought Keith. Must be a local expression for old people.

'Tourist got eaten by a crocodile only last month,' said Tracy.

Keith wished he hadn't mentioned rivers.

Then he remembered the forest, cool and green and alive with exotic birds.

'Just as well there's the forest,' he said. 'Bet it's paradise in there for a picnic.'

'Top spot on a hot day,' said Tracy. 'Cooler than an esky in there.'

Keith started to plan the picnic he'd take Mum and

Dad on at lunch-time.

'But you wouldn't actually sit down in there,' said Tracy. 'Mossies'd have their own picnic if you did. Plus there's the poisonous spiders and poisonous snakes. Great spot for a bushwalk but.'

Tracy then told Keith the story of her uncle's cousin's brother who'd been bitten by a snake in a phone box near a canefield and who'd been dead before he could ring for an ambulance.

Keith walked slowly back to the caravan.

'It'll be OK,' he said to himself.

It made him feel better so he said it again. A couple of hundred times.

Mum and Dad didn't have to know.

The important thing was to keep them cheerful so they could get a shop going and it could be a big success and they could all be happy.

All I've got to do, he decided, is keep them off the beach, out of rivers and out of the rain-forest.

And away from Tracy.

In the caravan Dad was making toast.

'Did you see Mum on your walk?' he asked.

Keith felt his stomach drop into the familiar bowl of cold batter.

Mum had already gone out.

She probably knew everything by now. At this very moment she was probably down on the beach listening to Tracy describe how a giant squid had eaten someone's grandfather.

Then Keith had a worse thought.

What if she'd gone for a paddle in a river?

He heard someone coming up the steps.

He couldn't look.

Who would it be? The police? A wheelchair salesman?

He looked.

It was Mum, with a big smile on her face.

'Guess what?' she said. 'I've found us a shop.'

TEN

It was the best-looking shop Keith had ever seen.

It was a more of a cottage than a shop, with a gleaming galvanised iron roof and fresh cream paint on the wooden walls and coloured plastic strips hanging in the doorway.

And it was a good ten yards from the nearest palm tree.

All it needs, thought Keith happily, is a sign on the front.

Paradise Fish Bar.

'Good position,' said Mum, pointing to the other shops nearby. 'General store, chemist, hardware, swimwear boutique and cake shop. Good assortment of customers and no direct competition.'

Dad looked up and down the dusty main street of Orchid Cove, then over the road at the beach.

For an awful moment Keith thought Dad had heard about the jellyfish.

'Should be some trade from the petrol station down on the corner,' said Dad.

Keith stopped holding his breath.

See, he said to himself, it's going to be all right.

Mum led them in through the coloured plastic

strips.

Keith looked around. The shop was dark and cool inside, and empty except for dusty shop fittings. Leaning against a wall were some old posters for something called a Chiko Roll.

'The woman who owns it retired last month,' said Mum. 'Sold all her stock and put the place up for rent.'

'What about equipment?' asked Dad.

'Fridge,' said Mum, pointing to a fridge. 'Sink,' she said, pointing to a sink. She pulled aside a pile of cardboard boxes. 'Fryer,' she said, pointing to a fryer. She gave Dad a grin. 'We're in business. We can be open in a week.'

Dad looked at her. 'What about the paperwork?'

'The place is still registered as a take-away food shop,' said Mum. 'Mrs McIntyre is happy for us to leave things as they are for now and when the renewal comes up we can change it over then.'

Dad looked doubtful.

'Look,' said Mum, 'if we're going to make a new life here, there's going to be lots of paperwork to sort out later on. First we've got to make the shop a success, right?'

'Right,' said Keith loudly.

Mum smiled and slipped her arm around Keith and gave him a squeeze.

They both looked at Dad, who was staring at the fryer with a gloomy face.

'Probably hasn't been serviced for ten years,' he said.

Don't think about that stuff, thought Keith. Don't. He'd given up telepathy but this was an emergency.

Mum grabbed Dad and turned him towards the window.

'Look,' she said, pointing across the road at the sea sparkling through the palm fronds. 'Does this look like the sort of place where fryers break down?'

Dad stared at the sea for a good minute.

If a jellyfish jumps out of the water now we've had it, thought Keith.

Then Dad turned back to them and rubbed his hands together.

'Let's get started,' he said. 'We've got a big job ahead of us.'

You're not kidding, thought Keith.

He hadn't checked under the shop for snakes yet.

While Mum started cleaning up the shop and Dad got on the phone to Cairns to order oil and potatoes and matzo flour, Keith checked under the shop for snakes.

The shop was built on wooden stumps, which meant he could walk around under it if he crouched low enough. It also meant he had room to swing the old machete he found hanging on one of the stumps.

He had to do that twice.

The first time was when he put his foot on a thirty-foot diamond-bellied black snake which he chopped into eight pieces before he saw the metal nozzle which connected it to the garden tap.

The second time was when he backed into a crocodile.

He felt its rough skin scrape the back of his legs.

Heart pounding, he slowly raised the machete, spun round, slipped, and sat down on the crocodile.

The crocodile had arm rests.

What a stupid place to leave an old vinyl settee, thought Keith. He sat back and waited for his heart to calm down.

He could hear Mum and Dad banging around above him with mops and brooms.

At least, he thought, they're too busy to be planning any picnics in the rain-forest or paddles at the beach.

He'd still hide their swimming costumes and the picnic plates, just in case.

The people of Orchid Cove were everything Keith had hoped they would be.

Cheerful.

Ron in the general store was cheerful. Charlie the chemist was cheerful. Doug at the petrol station was so cheerful you could hear him whistling even when he was taking wheel nuts off with a power tool.

Complete strangers were cheerful. They nodded to each other on the street and said 'G'day' and complemented each other on their new hats and cars and, in Keith's case, the new zinc cream on his nose. They said blue was a good choice of colour.

Only twice did Keith come across people in Orchid Cove who were not what he had hoped they would be.

The first time was early one morning, before Mum and Dad were awake, while Keith was making his daily circuit of the shower block, bashing the long grass with a stick to scare away snakes. (The caravan park owner had taken his machete away).

Suddenly, from one of the other caravans, Keith heard two people shouting at each other.

'I'm sick of this and I'm sick of you, you lazy, dirty pig,' shouted a woman's voice.

'Yeah well if I'm a pig,' shouted a man's voice, 'it's because this place is a pigsty.'

Keith went over and banged on the caravan door. It was opened by a man with a bare chest and a red face.

'Do you mind,' said Keith. 'There are plenty of big cities for that sort of thing. People have come here to be cheered up.'

The man scowled at him and slammed the door.

Later that day Keith spent some of Uncle Derek's going away money on a bunch of flowers and a bar of chocolate, which he left on the red-faced man's caravan step. It was what Mum and Dad gave each other when they'd been fighting and it seemed to work for them.

The second incident was in the hardware store when Keith was waiting to buy some tile adhesive for Dad.

The old man in front of Keith asked for twelve nails and a young assistant with pimples and a thin moustache rolled his eyes and made a sarcastic comment about building a new house.

Keith stepped forward

'If you do anything like that again,' he said to the assistant, 'I'll report you to the Far North Queensland

Tourist Office.'

The assistant stared at him, open-mouthed.

'Next time you feel grumpy,' said Keith, 'go out the back and read this.'

He pulled a comic from his back pocket and gave it to the startled assistant.

It was the only comic he'd brought from England, and he knew he was going to miss it, but it was for a good cause.

ELEVEN

'Opening Today' said the banner across the front of the shop.

Keith looked up at the banner proudly. Sixteen sheets of wrapping paper and two rolls of sticky tape and it was holding together perfectly.

He closed his eyes and made a wish.

I wish, he thought, that we get loads of customers and they all buy at least two bits of fish and none of them say anything about relatives who went for a paddle and never came back.

Then he went in through the coloured plastic strips and stood behind the counter with Mum and Dad.

He could tell they were nervous too.

Mum was going over the potatoes he'd peeled earlier, checking each one for eyes and bits of missed skin before she cut it into chips.

Keith watched her remove an eye that was so tiny an ant wouldn't have seen it without glasses.

Be fair, he thought, what do you expect for 4.13 cents a potato at the current rate of exchange?

Dad was battering fish more slowly and carefully than Keith had ever seen him do it.

Normally Dad floured and battered with short flicks

of the wrist that made Keith wonder why Dad didn't get a table-tennis table and have a crack at the world championships. This morning though, as Dad dragged each piece of fish carefully through the batter, he looked like he was playing the violin.

Keith caught himself having another quick glance at the fish. The vision flashed into his head again. The vision of their customers taking a bite of fish, screwing up their faces and dropping dead in the middle of reaching for the vinegar.

Stop it, he told himself. You're being silly. A fish co-op would not deliver stonefish or pufferfish for public consumption.

Then the plastic strips rattled and a man came into the shop.

Their first customer.

Keith gave him a big We-Don't-Know-You-Yet-But-We-Hope-You'll-Be-A-Regular-Customer smile.

Then Keith realised he did know him.

He felt the smile trickle off his face.

It was Mr Gambaso from the milk bar at the other end of the street.

And he was holding something behind his back.

Suddenly Keith had another vision. An argument with insults and shouting and hurtful comments about stealing customers and who was here first. Then Mr Gambaso brandishing the bread knife he was holding behind his back and running amok.

Keith prayed that Mr Gambaso wouldn't say who he was. That he'd just look around and leave quietly.

'Good morning,' said Mr Gambaso. 'I'm Joe Gambaso from the milk bar.'

That's it, thought Keith, we're goners.

'Morning,' said Dad. 'Vin Shipley. What can we do for you?'

'Just dropped in to wish you luck on your first day,' said Mr Gambaso. From behind his back he produced a soggy brown paper bag. 'I brought you a hamburger.'

He put it on the counter. They all looked at it.

'You er . . . you don't do hamburgers here, do you?' asked Mr Gambaso.

'No, we don't,' said Dad.

Mr Gambaso visibly relaxed.

'It's very kind of you,' said Mum. 'Vin, go on.' She pointed to the fryer.

Dad served up a fish and chips for Mr Gambaso.

'You er . . . you don't do fish and chips down at your place, Joe?' said Dad as he handed them over.

'No,' said Mr Gambaso.

Dad smiled and soon they were all munching away and chatting about cooking oils.

Phew, thought Keith as he watched them, that was a close one.

Their first real customer came in fifteen minutes later.

It was Doug from the petrol station.

'Morning tea,' he said with a big grin.

For a moment Keith thought Doug wanted a cup of tea and some biscuits. He could tell from their faces that Mum and Dad did too.

'If I don't have a decent feed for morning tea I'm

cactus by lunch,' said Doug with an even bigger grin. 'Two bits of fish and a dollar's worth of chips, thanks.'

When the order was cooked Dad tipped it into the paper and put it on the counter like he always did so the customer could do their own salt and vinegar.

Doug grabbed the bottle of tomato sauce that Mr Gambaso had warned them they should have on the counter and shook big puddles of it all over his fish and chips.

Keith stared.

'Vinegar?' asked Dad weakly.

'No, ta,' said Doug, 'I'm on a diet.'

Their next customer was the woman who worked in the chemist's. She introduced herself as Raylene and while her fish was in she told them about Mrs Newman in the post office's daughter's baby that could hum the theme to *Flying Doctors*.

Outside the shop Raylene stopped and ate a couple of mouthfuls and stuck her head back in through the plastic strips.

'Jeez,' she said, 'you Poms sure know how to make fish and chips.'

After that it seemed to Keith that most of Orchid Cove came in at some stage during the day. Even the hardware store assistant with the pimples and the thin moustache. He bought four lots of fish and chips, one with double salt, and gave Keith a motorbike magazine.

That evening Keith climbed slowly up the step-ladder and took the 'Opening Today' banner down.

His legs were aching but inside he felt like doing several cartwheels and a couple of handstands.

Fifty-three customers, eighty-one pieces of fish and not one mention of a snake or a sea wasp.

'G'day, Keith.'

Keith spun round.

In the dusk Tracy's skin looked browner than it had on the beach. Against all that brown her grin looked like a toothpaste advert, only crooked. At her feet was a small dog.

'This is Buster,' said Tracy. 'You didn't say you had a fish and chip shop.'

'It only opened today,' mumbled Keith. He couldn't take his eyes off the dog, which only had three legs and half an ear.

It looked like something had started to eat it and then spat it out. A crocodile? A jellyfish? A really big spider?

'You should have told me,' Tracy was saying. 'Mum would have got some for our tea.'

Keith mumbled that they were about to close up anyway. He glanced in the window. Mum and Dad were watching them, smiling.

Tracy was hunting through her pockets.

Don't go in and buy anything, please, thought Keith. If you go in they'll ask you about the dog.

'Skint,' said Tracy. 'Oh well.'

'Bye,' said Keith.

He started to go into the shop.

'Keith,' she said.

He stopped. Go home, he thought, please go home.

'The other morning, when I was telling you about Uncle Wal's cousin's brother who got bitten by the snake in the phone box, I didn't mean to make you feel crook. Sorry.'

Crook?

Whatever it meant, he wasn't going to admit to it.

'You didn't,' he said.

'Oh, good,' she said. 'It's just that when I said that bit about him being sick through his nose, I thought you went sorta pale. Dad's always saying I should leave that bit out, but I get carried away.'

'I was fine,' said Keith, feeling pale all over again.

He glanced in through the window and felt even paler.

Mum and Dad were coming out of the shop.

'Keith,' said Dad, 'Mum and me have been having a chat. It's been all work and no play since we got here so we've decided to go for a picnic on Saturday. Beach, rain-forest, wherever you like.'

'And we were wondering,' said Mum, smiling at Tracy, 'if your friend would like to come too?'

'Yeah,' said Tracy, grinning, 'I'd like that.'

TWELVE

'You burnt it down?'

Keith sighed.

He'd done that bit about five minutes ago. Some people's powers of concentration were pathetic.

Tracy was staring at him, the scab she'd been picking on her knee totally forgotten. Buster, curled up next to her in the old hammock, was staring at him too.

'I left the fryer on,' said Keith, 'and that burnt it down.'

'Jeez,' said Tracy, 'your parents must have been ropeable.'

Keith sighed again. He'd already explained how Mum and Dad had been upset and depressed, and angry if that's what ropeable meant.

'That's the whole point,' he said. 'They're happy now and they'll stay happy all the while they think this place is paradise.'

Tracy had gone back to picking her scab.

Great, thought Keith, here am I pouring out my innermost secrets to an almost complete stranger and she's not even listening.

Tracy's mum came out onto the verandah, the

weathered old boards creaking under her brown feet. She was holding two cans of drink.

'Guess what, Mum,' said Tracy. 'Keith burnt their fish and chip shop in England down.'

Keith sighed.

'I'm sure he didn't mean to,' said Tracy's mum, smiling at Keith. 'Lemonade or Fanta?'

Keith took the lemonade, thanked Tracy's mum and wished it was her who was coming on the picnic.

Tracy's mum went back inside.

When the wire screen door had stopped banging, Keith tried to continue.

'That's why I don't want them to know about the jellyfish and crocodiles and snakes and stuff. That's why we've got to find somewhere for the picnic that doesn't have any of those things.'

He looked up to see if Tracey understood now.

She wasn't even looking at him. She was watching a dusty car pull up next to the house. A man with hair as fair as hers got out of the car with a fishing rod in sections and a bucket.

'G'day, Dad,' said Tracy. 'This is Keith. He burnt their fish and chip shop in England down.'

'So,' said Tracy's dad, 'you're the Poms Trace has been telling us about. G'day.'

He held out his hand and Keith shook it.

Something didn't feel right. Keith realized he was only shaking three fingers and a thumb. There was a finger missing.

Perhaps, thought Keith, Tracy's dad and Buster had a fight and Buster bit off Tracy's dad's finger and

Tracy's dad bit off Buster's leg and half his ear.

It didn't seem likely.

He tried not to stare at the missing finger.

'If your dad likes fishing,' Tracy's dad was saying, 'send him round. They're biting real well at the moment.'

He showed them the bucket. Inside were three big pink fish.

'Or snorkelling,' he went on. 'Reef's a knockout if you haven't seen it. Better than telly.'

He ruffled Keith's hair and went inside.

Keith looked at Tracy.

'Do you understand about the picnic now?' he asked.

'He scratched it on some coral when he was seventeen,' said Tracy. 'It got infected and he had to have it chopped off.'

Keith took a deep breath.

'We've got to find somewhere for a picnic,' he said, 'with no crocodiles, no jellyfish, no snakes and no coral.'

The day of the picnic was very hot.

'So where's this surprise destination?' said Dad, locking up the door of the caravan. 'I bet it's the rainforest.'

'Stop it,' said Mum, wedging his new straw hat onto his head, 'it's a surprise. We'll find out when we get there.'

Keith grabbed one handle of Mum's shopping bag and waited for Dad to grab the other.

He wished the day was over and he was in bed.

No such luck.

Dad grabbed the other handle and they started walking towards the road, sandwiches rustling in greaseproof paper and bottles clinking.

'Have you always lived here, Tracy?' asked Mum.

'I was born here,' said Tracy. 'Well, not exactly here. We used to live inland a bit, near Crocodile Falls.'

Keith felt the blood drain from most of his body.

'Why's it called Crocodile Falls?' asked Dad.

This is it, thought Keith, in two seconds we'll be running back to the caravan.

''Cause the rocks at the bottom are so jagged,' said Tracy.

Thank God, thought Keith.

'Like teeth,' said Tracy.

Enough, thought Keith, don't go on.

He looked up and saw Tracy giving him a little grin.

They were almost at the beach.

'If we're going to the beach,' said Dad, 'I'll have to go back, I've forgotten my swimming trunks.'

'We're not going to the beach,' said Keith hastily. 'Tracy's got somewhere better.'

'It's along here,' said Tracy.

They walked along the road, past the shop, and kept on going.

'Hope it's not much further,' said Mum, 'it's getting a bit hot.'

'Nearly there,' said Tracy.

Keith had one more go at wishing the day was over and he was in bed.

Still no good.

Tracy led them into the grounds of the Orchid Cove Public School. They walked across the dusty playground and past the white wooden school building.

Behind the school was a playing field, mown into an oval and scorched yellow by the sun. In one corner was a metal climbing-frame. Tracy stopped next to it.

'Here we are,' she said. 'Don't climb on it, you'll burn your hands.'

'Isn't it a great spot?' said Keith. He unfolded the tarpaulin Tracy's dad had lent them and heaved it over the top of the climbing-frame.

'See,' he said, 'shade twenty-four hours a day.'

He and Tracy crawled inside and started unpacking the picnic things.

Keith risked a glance up at Mum and Dad.

Dad was staring as if he'd never seen a climbing-frame with a tarpaulin over it before.

Mum was looking a bit doubtful too. Then suddenly she grinned. And chuckled. And put her arm round Dad.

'They said it'd be a surprise,' she laughed. 'I'm surprised, are you surprised?'

Dad broke into a grin too. 'I'm very surprised,' he said.

Keith felt his heart start to slow down. He wondered if all this stress was going to catch up with him later in life.

Mum and Dad crawled in with them under the

tarpaulin and they all ate the sandwiches and drank the fizzy drinks while Tracy explained that this was the place where Russell Kinlock in Year Six had broken the world record for hanging upside down by his legs until a seagull had landed on him and he'd panicked and sprained his pelvis.

Mum and Dad roared with laughter.

Keith was delighted, even though he didn't see what was so funny. He'd sprained his ankle once and it had hurt like anything.

Then Tracy went out onto the oval and re-enacted Orchid Bay Public School winning the Far North Queensland Under-Twelves Softball Shield.

She did it all in slow-motion and had Mum and Dad in stitches.

Keith realised, as he watched her do a slow-motion diving catch, that he'd never met anyone like her before.

THIRTEEN

'No more, thanks Mrs Shipley,' said Tracy, flopping back against the caravan wall, 'I'm stuffed.'

Keith wasn't surprised.

Six pieces of cheese on toast she'd just had, four of them with tomato. And two pieces of fruit-cake.

Mum went to the other end of the caravan to turn the kettle down.

Keith leaned forwards across the fold-down table and whispered to Tracy.

'Thanks.'

She deserved it. Three hours at the picnic and an hour and a half at the tea table and she hadn't mentioned snakes or jellyfish once.

Keith realised Tracy was giving him a strange look. Probably indigestion.

'Great tea, but,' Tracy called out to Mum. 'Thanks for inviting me back.'

'Our pleasure, Tracy,' said Mum, 'I haven't laughed so much in years.'

'Me neither,' called Dad from outside. He was sitting on the caravan steps going through the first week's paperwork from the shop.

'What about you, Keith?' asked Mum. 'More cake?'

'No thanks,' said Keith.

'You've hardly eaten anything,' said Mum.

Keith gave Tracy a look which he hoped said 'Parents, couldn't you take them outside and bury them?'

When he thought about it, though, he had to admit Mum was right. He had hardly eaten anything. This must have been partly because he was laughing so much at Tracy's tales of life at Orchid Cove Public School, and partly because his stomach was knotted with excitement.

He had a plan.

It had come to him half-way through Tracy telling them about Mr Caulfield, a teacher who could do Donald Duck talk with his armpit.

Tracy's parents.

If Tracy could do it, be positive about Orchid Cove and not mention the bad stuff, perhaps her parents could too. And then Mum and Dad could make friends with them and spend evenings and weekends chatting with them on the verandah and never need to go to the beach or the rain-forest.

It was worth a try.

'Mum,' said Keith, 'you should meet Tracy's parents. They're great, aren't they, Tracy?'

Tracy smiled. 'Yeah, they're tops.'

'That would be very nice, Tracy,' said Mum.

'Yes,' said Dad, coming in from the steps, 'it would.'

So far so good, thought Keith.

Dad put his paperwork onto the table with a flourish.

'Well,' he said, grinning, 'looks like the shop's a goer.'

Mum gave him a delighted hug.

'Long way to go yet, of course,' continued Dad, 'but if we can keep the customers we've got so far, and get a few more as word spreads, I'd say we've got a successful shop on our hands.'

Keith looked at Mum and Dad's smiling faces and felt like rushing outside and howling at the moon with joy. Except that it might disturb the snakes.

Dad's expression turned serious. He looked at Mum and Keith.

'If it wasn't for you two,' he said, 'I'd still be sitting in South London with a long face.'

He kissed Mum and hugged Keith.

Keith glowed.

Dad turned to Tracy, grinning again. 'When Keith started going on about Australia, I thought he'd gone bonkers. And then Keith's mum started and I thought she had, too. But I came anyway and they were both right. It's paradise.'

Keith looked at Tracy, expecting her to be pretty pleased with what Dad had just said about her country.

Instead she stared down at the table.

Then she said, 'Thanks for tea, I'd better be going now.'

Tracy didn't say anything as Keith walked with her down to the road.

She seemed in a strange mood.

Keith decided it was definitely indigestion and thought he'd better leave off telling her his plan about her parents until another time.

'Do you want to come down to our shop tomorrow for some free fish and chips?' he said. 'There's something I want to talk to you about.'

It wasn't until he'd said it that he remembered about the six pieces of cheese on toast. Could be an expensive talk. Hundred potatoes at least.

'No, thanks,' she said, not looking up.

Keith stared at her.

'Why not?'

''Cause I don't want to see you any more.'

Keith couldn't believe what he was hearing.

'Why not?'

She turned to him angrily.

''Cause you're a whinger.'

Keith didn't know what that was but he felt sick in the stomach anyway.

'A what?'

'A whinger. OK, we've got a few crocs and stingers around here, so what? That's not the end of the bloody world.'

Keith realised what she meant. A whinger was a misery guts.

'You should learn to think positive,' she said, 'like your parents.'

Keith opened his mouth but nothing came out.

'Instead of being a whinging Pom,' Tracy said.

She walked away down the road.

After a bit she stopped and turned round.

'If you cheer up, give us a yell,' she shouted.

Then she kept on walking.

Keith watched her. He realised his eyes were stinging. He rubbed both of them hard.

A mosquito must have bitten him on both eyelids.

Later, in bed, Keith felt better.

Mum and Dad are happy, he thought, and that's the important thing. If they're happy, I'm happy.

He thought hard about whether he was happy.

He decided he was.

As he went to sleep, he tried not to think about what a great friend Tracy would have been.

FOURTEEN

Keith struggled awake.

A noise. On the roof of the caravan. Drumming. Rumbling. Thumping.

Snakes fighting?

A crocodile demanding to be let in?

Suddenly he knew what it was.

Rain.

Rain? Less than twelve hours ago, at the picnic, it had been searingly hot and there hadn't been a cloud in the sky.

He sat up in the darkness and pulled the curtain aside. Water was running down the outside of the window.

Think.

It could be a lawn sprinkler that had come on by mistake. Perhaps that couple in the other caravan had had another fight and one of them had switched on the lawn sprinkler to sprinkle the other.

Keith peered over towards the shower block floodlight. In the arc of light he could see millions of drops of water falling from much higher up than a lawn sprinkler could sprinkle.

Rain.

Panic gripped him in the chest.

How could he do anything about rain?

Even if Tracy's parents were the best actors in the world they couldn't keep Mum and Dad shut up in their living-room with the curtain drawn and the telly turned up for ever.

Sooner or later Mum and Dad would step outside and there it would be. Grey skies. Grey buildings. Rain.

And gradually, drip by drip, Mum's forehead would pucker up and Dad's mouth would droop and the customers would stop coming and the shop would go broke and they'd be reduced to living on river banks and fighting with crocodiles over scraps of rotting take-away chicken . . .

Keith clenched his fists.

Think positive.

If the sky was blue twelve hours ago, this must be a freak storm that's blown in from somewhere close that has rain. New Zealand. China. Somewhere like that.

And if it's blown in, thought Keith, stands to reason it'll blow out again. Probably by morning. When Mum and Dad wake up, the sky'll probably be blue again.

Not probably, it will be.

And Mum and Dad'll never know anything about it.

As long as they don't wake up now.

Keith held his breath and listened for their breathing. He couldn't hear anything except the drumming of the rain.

He felt on the floor next to his bed and found the candle and matches Mum had left there in case of emergency.

The candle flame lit up the caravan with a flickering yellow light.

Keith slipped out of bed and gently pulled aside the curtain that hung between Mum and Dad's bed and his.

Mum and Dad were both asleep.

Keith silently thanked the traffic of South London for turning them into such heavy sleepers.

But the rain on the roof was getting louder.

He couldn't chance it.

He found Mum's make-up bag, pulled out some tufts of cotton-wool, rolled them into little balls, and carefully, gently, holding his breath, pushed one into one of Mum's ears.

She stirred slightly but stayed asleep.

He eased one into her other ear.

Dad was harder to do because he was on the other side of the bed.

Keith leaned over Mum, praying she wouldn't wake up and scream.

The first ball fell out of Dad's ear. Too small. He made bigger ones and eased them in.

Done.

He straightened up, heart pounding.

Now, check to make sure all the windows are closed.

That's when he remembered.

The side window in the shop.

He'd left it open so the shop wouldn't be too hot on

Monday morning.

A night of pounding rain and the shop could be awash. Electrical wires could short-circuit. There could be a fire.

Another one.

He stood there, sweating, in the flickering candlelight.

I'll have to do it, he thought. I'll have to go and shut that window.

He was drenched to the skin before he got to the bottom of the caravan steps.

So much for Mum's showerproof raincoat.

He clasped it round him and sloshed across the caravan park, slipping in the mud, eyes almost closed against the rain that beat on his head and shoulders like stones.

Blimey, he thought, this is worse than Worthing.

Then he reached the road.

For a moment Keith thought he'd been slammed in the back with a plank of wood, then he realised it was wind, screaming at him out of the darkness.

He staggered across the road and was only able to stop when he came up against the rough brick wall of the milk bar.

The rain was coming at him sideways now, and it felt like it was going to rip Mum's showerproof raincoat to shreds.

Keith squinted towards the beach.

All he could see were huge black waves pounding in, and foam being torn off them by the wind. Forget

Worthing, he thought, this is worse than Scarborough.

He started to edge his way towards the shop at the other end of the street, eyes almost closed, the wind flattening him against the buildings as he struggled along.

Just past the hardware store he took another painful squint at the beach.

And saw the palm trees.

No longer were they leaning gracefully over the sand, they were thrashing around, fronds flailing in the black sky.

Suddenly it hit him.

Coconuts.

Fortunately it was only the thought that hit him. The coconut itself, the first of them, slammed against the post office wall in front of him and exploded.

Keith saw that the road was littered with coconuts. He heard others smashing into wood and glass.

Run, he thought. Leg it. Go back.

Then he remembered the shop.

If he didn't save the shop, there was no point in going back.

He hunched over and put his left arm up between him and the thrashing palm trees and edged forward.

A car with only one headlight and no windscreen went slowly past and the driver shouted something at him but Keith kept his head down and kept going.

Another coconut exploded against the wall in front of him.

A rubbish bin flew past his head.

Then he realised he was outside the swimwear

boutique which meant the next shop was theirs. He peered ahead. There it was.

He heard a screeching, groaning noise above him. He looked up and saw that the metal roof of the swimwear boutique was flapping around like a bedspread. It was coming down, towards him.

He flung himself against the wall as the sheets of tin crashed onto the road and were hurled along it, sparks flying.

And then suddenly the sheets of metal were in the air again and smashing, two and three at a time, into the front of the Paradise Fish Bar.

Keith watched the front of the shop disappear as the wind picked up the shattered glass and splintered wood and twisted metal and whipped them away.

He stared, numb, as the next gust, thundering into the open front of the shop, blew out every other window in the building.

He stood leaning against the swimwear boutique wall until the feeling came back into his body.

Paradise, he thought, looking at the dark, howling beach.

Rain and sand stung his eyes and he didn't care.

Twelve thousand miles, five airlines, seventy-three hours.

And all you had to do was make us happy.

'Thanks a lot, paradise,' he yelled, 'thanks a bleeding lot.'

He yelled it again, screaming it into the wind with great sobs. He was still yelling it when the real plank of wood slammed into him and everything went black.

FIFTEEN

First he saw Mum's face, looking down at him with sad red-rimmed eyes and wet cheeks and her forehead screwed up into so many criss-cross lines he felt dizzy and sick trying to count them.

Then he saw Dad's face, frowning at him with dark eye bulges and droopy mouth creases that were darker and droopier than he'd ever seen before.

Then he saw Mitch Wilson, staring at him gloomily.

Then he saw Owen the milkman, looking at him sadly.

Then he saw Mr Naylor, smiling at him with a thin mocking smile and drinking orange paint.

Then he woke up.

He was in a bed in a big bright room with lots of other beds in it.

Mum and Dad were sitting by the bed looking down at him.

Mum smiled, but her frown lines didn't go away.

Dad smiled too, but his droopy mouth creases just sort of stretched a bit.

They both hugged him.

Keith realised he had a headache.

'You're in hospital in Cairns, love,' said Mum gently.

'You're going to be OK,' said Dad.

They told him about the storm and how it was the edge of a cyclone that had gone back out to sea and how Raylene from the chemist's had found him lying unconscious in the road on her way to check that Mrs Newman was OK and how the ambulance had taken hours to get him to Cairns because the road was blocked by trees and how he'd been asleep for eighteen hours and how worried they'd been about him.

Keith didn't say anything about the shop because they didn't and he thought they looked depressed enough after sitting on those hard hospital chairs for eighteen hours.

He didn't mention it in the days that followed, either.

He decided not to say much about anything.

He slept most of the time, and when he wasn't asleep he pretended he was so he wouldn't have to talk to Mum, who sat by his bed for several hours each day.

He wanted to talk, but not about the things he thought she'd want to talk about.

Like how coming to Australia was the worst thing they'd ever done and how they'd be going back to England as soon as Keith was better.

Anyway, she didn't have to tell him that out loud. He could tell from her face.

On the third day he couldn't stand it any more and

spoke.

'Nurse,' he said, 'could you get my mum a cushion?'

The only cheery person around was the doctor who stopped by the bed each day and shone a light into Keith's eyes.

'Good,' he said every day, 'good. I wish the plank of wood was coming along as well as you.'

Then one day Mum came in looking much happier.

'Come on,' she said, 'we're going home today.'

'Where's Dad?' asked Keith.

'At home,' said Mum.

Great, thought Keith, Dad was so anxious to get back to Owen the milkman he couldn't even wait for us.

As Keith got dressed, he wondered if people who'd had concussion were allowed to fly.

Perhaps they won't let me on the plane, he thought.

Then Mum would have to fly to England without him and he'd stay in Australia and become a wealthy sheep farmer with a property the size of Lewisham and then he could fly them back out.

Forget it, he thought gloomily. Champion boxers fly all the time and they get concussion on a weekly basis.

As he climbed into the ambulance Keith briefly considered making a run for it, but decided not to.

He didn't fancy being on the run in a country where the police carried guns and chewed chewing-gum.

What's the point, he thought glumly. Lie back and let it happen.

He'd tried to make Mum and Dad happy and it hadn't worked out.

At least he'd have the consolation, when they were living in a high-rise council flat and Dad was selling roof insulation and they were all miserable, of knowing he'd tried.

Keith wondered why the ambulance was taking so long to get to the airport. He tried to see if they were in a traffic jam but couldn't because of the frosted glass in the windows.

He looked at Mum, dozing in her seat, and remembered how her face had lit up when she first saw Orchid Cove.

And how she'd smiled when Dad had announced the shop was a goer.

Now, as she dozed, not only was her brow furrowed, her mouth was starting to droop too.

'Mum,' he said.

She blinked awake. 'Yes, dear?'

'I've got something to tell you.'

'What's that, love?'

Keith took a deep breath. This wasn't going to be easy but it might just make her feel a bit better about having to leave.

'There are poisonous jellyfish,' he said. 'In the sea off Orchid Cove. And all up and down the coast.'

'I know, love,' she said.

Keith had already started telling her about the

stonefish before he realised what she'd said.

She knew?

'Stonefish,' she was saying, 'that's right.'

'And crocodiles in the rivers,' he said, wondering if he was dreaming.

'I know,' she said, smiling.

'And poisonous snakes,' he said.

'That's right,' she said.

'And spiders,' he said, suddenly desperate to find at least one horrible thing she didn't know about.

'Yes,' she said.

'And coconuts that drop on your head and coral that infects your fingers,' he shouted.

Mum bit her lip.

At last, thought Keith, something.

'I'm sorry, love,' said Mum, 'we should have told you about all those things.'

Keith stared at her.

'But we knew how much you wanted this place to be perfect,' she continued, 'and we didn't want to make you miserable.'

Keith tried to speak but couldn't.

'We should have told you,' said Mum, 'when Uncle Derek's travel agent friend told us.'

'So you mean,' said Keith with difficulty, 'you don't mind about them?'

Mum smiled and shook her head.

Keith's head was spinning.

'So if the cyclone hadn't come,' he said, 'we wouldn't be leaving?'

Mum looked at him with a puzzled little frown.

'Leaving?' she said. 'We're not leaving.'

Keith realised the ambulance had come to a stop and the driver had turned the engine off.

The doors opened and Keith could smell fish and chips.

He stepped out.

They were in Orchid Cove.

The ambulance was parked in front of the shop.

The shop had a new front on it.

Keith could smell the primer on the new timber. Through the new panes of glass he could see Dad at the fryer, hair curled up at the front.

Dad saw him and came out.

'Not a bad job, eh?' said Dad, pointing to the new front of the shop. 'Mind you, I had expert help.'

Out of the shop came Doug from the service station and Tracy's dad and Tracy, all eating fish and chips.

'G'day,' said Tracy. 'Your dad's been telling me some of the things you used to get up to in England. Pretty wild stuff for a Pommy whinger.'

Grinning, she offered him a chip.

Dazed, he took one.

'They reckon,' Dad was saying, 'that cyclones only come once in a blue moon, so we've decided not to worry about the next one till it happens.'

Keith stared at Mum and Dad.

Grinning, they both gave him a hug.

'OK,' said Dad, 'enough of this. There's a shop to be painted. We've saved you the top coat.'

He handed Keith a paint-brush and a tin of paint.

Keith looked at the brush and the tin. Then he

looked back at Mum and Dad, whose grins had become huge smiles of delight. They gazed at him, eyes shining.

Keith realised he was feeling something he hadn't felt for a very long time.

He was feeling happy.

He dipped the brush into the Tropical Mango Hi-Gloss.

Now read the next part of
Keith's adventure in
Worry Warts...

WORRY WARTS

For Chris, Sophie and Ben

ONE

The trouble with tropical paradises, thought Keith as he sprinted out of the school building, is that everyone's too relaxed.

He swerved to avoid a year four kid strolling along sucking a mango, leapt over a group of year three's sprawled under the palm trees swapping shells, and glanced at his watch.

Sixteen minutes past three.

Only two hours and forty-nine minutes left.

Thanks a lot Mr Gerlach, thought Keith bitterly. There ought to be a law against teachers being that relaxed. Yakking on for thirteen minutes after the bell. Couldn't he see when a person's guts were in knots because a person was running out of time?

Keith hurtled out of the school gate, skidded to avoid a year five kid trying to crack a coconut with a recorder, and sprinted along the dusty street towards the shops. He glanced at his watch again.

Two hours and forty-eight minutes left.

Would it be enough?

He felt the knot tightening in his guts.

Calm down, he thought. I'll be OK as long as Mrs Newman in the post office doesn't start yakking on about her grandson.

Mrs Newman in the post office started yakking on about her grandson.

'Only seventeen months old,' she said to Keith, 'and he can say prawn.'

Pick up the savings book, thought Keith. Pick it up.

Mrs Newman picked up Keith's savings book from the counter.

'Gee,' she said, looking at the withdrawal slip, 'thirty-eight dollars. Are you sure you want to take all that out in one go?'

No, thought Keith, I want a one cent coin every Friday for the next fourteen thousand years.

'Yes,' said Keith. 'And I'm in a bit of a hurry thanks.'

He glanced up at the post office clock.

Two hours and forty-one minutes left.

'That only leaves one dollar and twenty-seven cents in your account,' said Mrs Newman.

'That's right,' said Keith.

'Must be for something important, thirty-eight dollars,' said Mrs Newman.

'It is,' said Keith.

'That's good,' she said, 'cause it'd be a shame to take out thirty-eight dollars and just fritter it away.'

'Mrs Newman,' said Keith, 'I had to peel seven hundred and sixty potatoes to earn that money. I'm not going to fritter away seven hundred and sixty potatoes.'

Mrs Newman smiled and started writing slowly in his savings book.

Keith looked up at the clock again. Two hours and forty minutes left.

Mrs Newman stopped writing.

Oh no, thought Keith. Please don't ask me how I'm liking Australia. Not again. I haven't got time.

'How are you liking Australia?' asked Mrs Newman.

'Fine thanks,' said Keith, making a mental note to write to the council and ask when Orchid Cove would be getting an automatic bank machine.

Mrs Newman wrote a couple more numbers, then stopped and looked up again. 'Tell your mum and dad I'm sorry I couldn't get in for my fish and chips yesterday, but Gail had to get her feet done and I had Shaun and Alex so we had baked beans. How are your mum's feet?'

'Fine thanks,' said Keith, sighing.

'The trouble with North Queensland,' said Mrs Newman, 'is that your feet swell up.'

The trouble with North Queensland, thought Keith, is that everyone's too friendly.

He glanced at his watch.

Two hours and thirty-nine minutes left.

No need to panic, he thought. I'll be OK as long as there's not a queue in the hardware store.

Keith stood in the queue in the hardware store and started to panic.

Two hours and thirty-two minutes left.

He was running out of time.

Relax, he told himself. It's only a short queue, just Gary Murdoch and his dad. They can't need that much hardware cause they only moved into their new house three weeks ago.

'Tap washers,' said Mr Murdoch to the assistant. 'You wouldn't credit it. Brand new place, all the taps are dripping.'

Keith's heart sank. Gary had been boasting all week in class about how his new house had twenty-seven taps. This could take ages.

'How many?' asked the assistant.

Mr Murdoch started counting in his head.

'Twenty-seven,' said Keith.

Gary and Mr Murdoch both turned round.

'G'day Keith,' said Gary. 'Dad, this is Keith Shipley, the kid I was telling you about.'

'G'day,' said Mr Murdoch, looking down at Keith with a grin. 'You're the bloke dragged his parents out here from pommyland to cheer 'em up, right?'

'I didn't drag them,' said Keith, 'they agreed to come.'

'Only after you burnt half the street down, but, eh?' said Gary.

'It was just one fish and chip shop and it was an accident,' said Keith, hoping the dripping tap in Gary Murdoch's ensuite bathroom flooded his bedroom and made his Walkman go rusty.

'Has it worked?' asked Mr Murdoch. 'Have they cheered up?'

'Actually,' said Keith, 'if you don't mind I'm in a bit of a hurry.'

'There,' said the assistant, scooping a pile of washers into a bag, 'twenty-seven.'

Mr Murdoch ignored him. He looked hard at Keith. 'Bowls,' he said. 'Get 'em to join the bowls club, that'll cheer 'em up. And if they're having a house built, tell 'em to watch the taps.'

The trouble with tropical paradises, thought Keith, glancing at his watch, is that everyone's too helpful.

Keith sprinted out of the hardware store, paint cans thumping together in his school bag.

The clock on the war memorial across the street said eight minutes past eleven. Keith stared. Then he remembered it had been wrong ever since a coconut had hit it in the cyclone.

He looked at his watch. Nineteen minutes to four. Two hours and twenty-four minutes left.

He should just make it.

As long as Mum and Dad didn't see him.

Keith decided he'd better not risk going too close to the shop so he ran across the road, through the fringe of palm trees and on to the beach. He ran along the soft sand, trying to look like a tourist out for a jog with a couple of tins of paint in his school bag.

He glanced through the palm trees at the shop.

Mum and Dad were both behind the counter but neither of them was looking in his direction. They were looking at each other. Dad was saying something to Mum, pointing at her with a piece of fish, and Mum was saying something back, waving the chip scoop at him.

Even at that distance, Keith could see that Dad's mouth was droopier than a palm frond and that

Mum's forehead had more furrows in it than wet sand when the sea was a bit choppy.

Keith's stomach knotted even tighter.

Another argument.

Poor things. Stuck in a fish and chip shop all day in this heat. Anyone'd get a bit irritable standing over a fryer all day with this poxy sun pounding down non-stop.

The trouble with tropical paradises, thought Keith as he ran on along the beach, is that there's too much good weather.

He went back up to the road and crossed it at the spot where the bus from the airport had dropped them four months earlier.

He remembered Mum and Dad's faces, aglow with huge smiles as they saw Orchid Cove for the first time.

All they need is a bit of cheering up again, thought Keith as he sprinted towards the house. Which is exactly what they'll get when they arrive home in two hours and twenty-one minutes.

TWO

Keith looked at his watch. Forty-seven minutes left and he'd almost finished.

Not bad going, he thought, considering it's the first time I've ever painted a car.

He crouched down to do a bit he'd missed at the bottom of a wheel arch, and noticed that one of the back tyres was a bit flat.

Stands to reason, he thought. Sitting out here in front of the house for weeks without being driven.

While he did around the number plate he tried to remember the last Sunday they'd gone for a drive. Was it the time they went down to Mission Beach and Dad dropped his ice-cream and they all had a good laugh and then Mum got a migraine? Or was it the day they went to the crocodile farm and Mum insisted on having lunch in the café there and Dad got the trots?

Keith couldn't remember.

Anyway, he thought, as he finished off the exhaust pipe, it was before Mum took up Sunday bush walking and Dad took up Sunday crosswords. Which hadn't fooled Keith for a moment. He knew exactly why Mum and Dad didn't want to go out for Sunday drives anymore.

They were embarrassed.

Embarrassed to be seen driving around in an off-white 1979 Toyota Corolla with rust spots when Gary Murdoch's dad had a bright-red 1990 Mercedes with speed stripes and chrome wheels.

Well you won't have to be embarrassed anymore, thought Keith.

He put a second coat on the dent Mum had made in the passenger door the day she flung it open and hit a steel girder.

Keith shuddered as he remembered that day.

They'd been parked in the drive-in bottle shop. Mum and Dad had been arguing about which beer to buy.

The trouble with tropical paradises, thought Keith as he put a third coat on the dent, is that there are too many brands of beer.

'Jeez.'

Keith turned at the sound of the familiar voice.

Tracy stood there looking at the car.

'It's a bit bright, but,' she said.

That's a good one, thought Keith, coming from a girl with a luminous orange and purple skateboard. And pink patches on her face where the brown was peeling off.

'It's a wedding anniversary present for my mum and dad,' he said.

'Hope you got them sunglasses as well,' said Tracy.

A twinge of panic hit Keith under the ribs. Perhaps it was a bit bright. The Tropical Mango he'd painted

8

the shop in England with had been a bit bright and they hadn't liked that at first.

Relax, he told himself, this is different. Mum and Dad were misery guts then. Now they're cheerful, adventurous globe-trotters who are just feeling the heat a bit. Don't be a worry wart.

The panic went as he remembered how Dad had stared enviously the first time Mr Murdoch had driven past in his bright-red Mercedes.

'Do they know about it?' asked Tracy.

'It's a surprise,' he said.

'It'll be a surprise all right,' said Tracy, 'when they find they've got the only green car with yellow stripes in the whole of Far North Queensland.'

'It's not green and yellow,' said Keith, 'it's Tropical Parrot and Hot Sunflower. And they're speed stripes.'

'Gary Murdoch's dad'll chuck his guts with envy when he sees that,' said Tracy, grinning at him.

Keith grinned back. Good old Tracy. You could trust a mate to say the right thing.

'What made you choose green and yellow?' asked Tracy.

'I wanted it to be Mum and Dad's favourite colours,' said Keith, 'so I checked out their wardrobe. Mum's got three separate things that are green and yellow stripes and Dad's got a yellow shirt and green socks.'

'Jeez, you're a clever mongrel,' said Tracy.

Keith glowed. When some kids said that they were sending you up, but when Tracy said it you knew she meant it.

'Is this why you nicked off after school without hanging around for softball?' she asked.

'Sorry,' said Keith, 'I was on a tight deadline. I only had the idea in art. Had to make sure I got it finished before Mum and Dad got home from the shop.'

'They don't get home for another forty minutes,' said Tracy.

'Thirty-nine,' said Keith, 'thirty-eight if they walk fast.'

'Jeez, you're a worry wart,' said Tracy, grinning at him again.

He asked her whether she thought he should do the bumper bars to disguise the dent where Dad had backed into a concrete post in the Cairns car-park the day Mum had bought her green and yellow striped swimming costume.

Tracy said she reckoned he should leave them in case his mum bought some more expensive clothes and his dad backed into something else, which would only chip the paint.

Keith agreed.

'Gotta go now,' said Tracy, 'gotta help clean out the chooks. See you down the beach later?'

'Maybe,' said Keith.

He didn't want to be more definite because there was always the chance that when Mum and Dad saw the paint job they'd want Keith to leap straight into the car with them and drive up to Port Douglas to have a pizza in the outdoor restaurant under the fairy lights, where they'd all clink their glasses together, or their metal containers if they were having milkshakes, and toast their happiness together for ever and ever.

One minute to go.

Keith did a final check. Camera. Anniversary card. Ribbon.

He hoped Mum and Dad wouldn't mind about the ribbon. He hadn't been able to find one long enough to go round a car. The clothes-line looked OK anyway, even if the bow was a bit floppy.

The anniversary card looked great, standing on the bonnet. Now it was painted you couldn't see it was made from bits of Chicko Roll boxes. The Hot Sunflower *Happy Wedding Anniversary* stood out really well against the Tropical Parrot.

He checked round the car for drips.

Hardly any.

It had really paid off, using quick-drying plastic paint. Much better than the gloss stuff he'd used on the shop in England, which had taken a week to dry just because there'd been a bit of rain.

Keith glanced at his watch.

Six minutes past six.

Where were they?

Perhaps they were still at the shop arguing and they hadn't noticed the time.

Keith tried to force that awful thought out of his mind.

He still hadn't managed to when Mum and Dad came round the corner.

Keith took a deep breath.

'Happy wedding anniversary,' he shouted, squinting into the camera.

He wanted to get their faces the moment they broke into huge glowing grins.

Through the viewfinder he could see them moving towards him, eyes wide and mouths open.

Come on, thought Keith, let's have the delighted smiles.

'Happy wedding anniversary,' he shouted again.

Mum and Dad were very close now, eyes still wide and mouths still open.

Come on, thought Keith, smile or you'll be out of focus.

He pressed the button anyway, just as Mum started to cry.

After Dad had taken Mum into the house, Keith stared at the car for a long while, trying to think.

Why hadn't they said anything about the paint job?

Because they hadn't needed to, probably. Tears from Mum and a mouth drooping almost to the ground from Dad had said it all.

They didn't like it.

Keith felt his eyes getting hot.

Pull yourself together, he thought. Be positive. Why don't they like it?

The colours?

The unpainted bumper bars?

The fact that I only put one 'n' in 'anniversary'?

No problem, he said to himself.

If they're worried about my spelling I'll do extra homework.

If they're upset about the bumper bars I'll paint them.

If they don't like Tropical Parrot and Hot Sunflower I'll have the whole car another colour by tomorrow night. Off-white if they want.

Suddenly he felt much better.

Trust Mum and Dad to make a big drama out of such a simple problem, whichever one it was.

Keith went into the house, working out how many kids he'd have to borrow a dollar from to buy two litres of off-white paint.

Mum and Dad were in their bedroom, talking.

Keith didn't mean to listen, but their voices came clearly through the thin wall.

'We can't carry on like this,' said Mum's voice tearfully.

'What about Keith?' said Dad's voice.

Keith was shocked. Dad's voice sounded like he'd been crying too.

'Plenty of kids' parents split up,' said Mum's shaking voice, 'it's not the end of the world.'

Keith stood in the narrow, hot hallway and the blood pounded in his ears so loudly that he thought for a few seconds another cyclone had hit.

Then he ran out of the house.

THREE

Keith didn't stop running till he got to the beach. He threw himself down on the sand under a palm tree and squeezed his eyes shut.

He wished he could open them and find himself back in England, even somewhere boring like Watford or Lancashire, just so long as things were back to normal and there was a fish and chip shop with Mum and Dad in it, with only slightly miserable faces, together, as usual.

Or France. Or Russia.

Anywhere, he thought bitterly, except this poxy so-called tropical paradise.

He stared up at the sunset. The sky was rippled with pink and orange and purple. It looked like the time Ryan Garner pinched nine packets of lollies and threw up on the monkey bars.

The darkening air was loud with the screech of insects. Cicadas being negative. Mosquitoes being defeatist. Grasshoppers lying to their kids about the state of their marriage.

Keith felt hot tears.

'Shut up,' he shouted at the grasshoppers.

He took a deep breath. The tropical evening smells made him feel sick. He could smell rotting fruit and

squashed cane toads and poisonous flowers that para-
lysed their victims with squirts of rancid liquid. Probably their kids too.

For the hundredth time since running out of the
house he tried to think of something else that Mum
could have been saying.

Something other than split up.

He couldn't.

He stared at the ocean. The waves were pink and
frothy and looked like toothpaste that had been spat
out by someone with a bleeding gum.

He thought about what was probably going on
under the water. Stonefish not talking to each other.
Pufferfish having arguments and getting migraines.
Killer jellyfish splitting up and emotionally neglecting
their kids.

The hot tears wouldn't stop.

I wish, thought Keith, I'd never brought Mum and
Dad to this poxy, stinking, rat-hole of a dump.

They were OK in England. Misery guts, yes, but a
holiday would have fixed that.

Wait a sec.

A holiday.

Suddenly his mind was racing.

He tried to remember the last time Mum and Dad
had been on holiday.

Five years ago?

Ten?

Being in this dump didn't count. All they were doing
here was what they used to do in England, slaving
over a fryer and a bowl of batter, and being miserable.

Except here it was worse because they were in a poxy, overheated, so-called tropical paradise.

No wonder they were getting irritable and stressed and imagining they didn't want to be together any more.

A holiday, that's what they needed.

Keith scrambled to his feet, tears gone, heart pounding with excitement.

He needed some holiday details fast and he knew just where to get them.

'There you go,' said Tracy, 'take your pick.'

She dropped the last bundle of brochures on to her bed.

Keith stared.

There were thousands.

He'd seen bits of Tracy's travel brochure collection before, but never the whole lot at once.

'OK,' said Tracy, 'this bundle is adventure holidays, this one is mountain ranges, this is old cities, this is modern cities, this is campsites with views, this is campsites without views, this is relics of ancient civilizations, this is cruises, this is traditional villages in remote valleys untouched by the modern world, this is places that are flat but interesting, and this is tropical paradises, except you probably won't want that one.'

Dead right, thought Keith as he dropped to his knees and grabbed the first bundle.

A thought hit him. Probably better to stick to this end of the world. That way Mum and Dad won't feel they've wasted their money coming all the way down here.

He told Tracy this and she explained that the Australia and New Zealand brochures were at the back of each bundle.

He started pulling out brochures.

'You're sure she said split up?' asked Tracy, kneeling down next to him. 'Mr Gambaso in the milk bar sold my dad a hamburger once with a bit of bone in it and Dad broke a filling and said he'd kill him. I was on the roof chasing cane toads and I freaked and hid his fish-gutting knife. Turned out he'd said he'd bill him.'

'Mum said it,' replied Keith, 'but she didn't mean it. She's under stress.'

'I know what you mean,' said Tracy. 'I told my mum I was gunna be a nun once just cause she wouldn't let me watch Bugs Bunny.'

Keith moved on to the next bundle.

'If they do split up,' said Tracy, 'which one'll you live with?'

Sometimes, thought Keith, even mates say the wrong thing.

'Or is that why you want the brochures,' continued Tracy, 'so you can choose the one who's planning to take the most interesting holidays? I'd pick the one who wants to go to Venice. I'd eat bricks to go to Venice. Or Peru. Or Melbourne.'

She slumped back against the bed and stared dreamily at a poster of the Victorian Arts Centre on the wall.

'Melbourne sounds great,' she said. 'Anywhere sounds great when you've never been further than Proserpine.'

Before Keith could explain that the brochures were for a second honeymoon for Mum and Dad so they could rediscover how deeply in love they were and never think about splitting up ever again, Tracy's mum came in with two cans of lemonade.

'Tracy ear-bashing you about her travel dreams, is she?' grinned Tracy's mum to Keith. She winked at Tracy.

'If you and Dad split up,' said Tracy, 'I'd pick Dad cause at least he'd go to Venice for the fishing.'

Keith nearly choked on a mouthful of lemonade. He wished Tracy would change the subject.

'I want to travel,' said Tracy's mum indignantly. 'When we've got a new roof and had the house re-stumped and saved up for an air-conditioner for the lounge, I'll be off for a week in Proserpine like a shot.'

'Rack off, you boring old chook,' said Tracy. Even though she and her mum were both grinning, Keith was shocked.

Dad called out the moment Keith stepped in through the fly screen door.

'Keith, in here.'

Mum and Dad were in the lounge, Mum on the settee next to the fan and Dad standing in the corner.

'Keith,' said Dad, 'we're very angry about the car.'

Keith looked at them.

They didn't look angry, they looked sad.

Mum's eyes were red and she'd rolled the *TV Times* into a tight tube and was gripping it with both hands. Her forehead was more corrugated than the dirt road out to Meninga.

Both corners of Dad's mouth were pointing to the floor and so were both his shoulders.

'We're very angry and disappointed,' said Dad.

'Is it the colours or the bumper bars or the spelling?' asked Keith in a small voice.

Dad's eyebrows went lower and now he did look angry.

'It's because you didn't discuss it with us first,' he said, his voice suddenly louder.

'I'm sorry,' said Keith miserably, 'I wanted to surprise you.'

'We know you did, love,' said Mum, 'and it was a lovely thought, but you should have talked to us about it first.'

'I can fix it up,' said Keith. 'If it's the Tropical Parrot and Hot Sunflower you don't like, I can fix that. Have a look at these, and I'll have it repainted any colour you like by the time you get back.'

He thrust a wad of holiday brochures at each of them.

'There's a great motel in Hobart,' he said as Mum and Dad stared at the brochures. 'It's on a hill and at this time of the year the winds down there have already started. It'll be freezing. You'll love it.'

Now they were both staring at him, mouths open.

'How about Adelaide?' said Keith. 'The Barossa

Valley's great for bush walks and crosswords and they get heaps of rain at this time of year.'

Dad stared at the brochures again and then at Keith again. 'For God's sake,' he said, 'we can't think about holidays, we've got a shop to run.'

'It's OK,' said Keith, 'I've worked it out. I'll take a couple of weeks off school and Tracy can help during the tea-time rush. She knows her way round a fish from going snorkelling with her dad. And Gino Morelli can help too, his dad used to run the aquarium in . . .'

'Keith,' Dad broke in, 'we are not going on any holiday.'

'It's a nice idea,' said Mum, 'but it's just not possible.'

'You've got to,' said Keith. 'How about a hang-gliding holiday in New Zealand? You go up to the snowfields in a helicopter, and you can bungy-jump too if you want.'

'We are not,' thundered Dad, 'going on holiday.'

'But you've got to,' pleaded Keith.

'Why have we?' asked Mum.

Keith took a deep breath. He had to say it.

'So you can stop talking about splitting up.'

There was a long silence.

Mum and Dad exchanged a look.

Keith's insides felt like they were in a spin-dryer.

Then Dad stepped forward and put his hands on Keith's shoulders and spoke slowly and softly.

'If you've heard us saying anything about splitting up, it's not what you think. We've been talking about splitting up in the shop, that's all.'

There was another long silence.

Keith struggled to work out what Dad meant, but his head felt like it was full of uncooked batter.

'What Dad's saying,' said Mum softly, 'is that the shop isn't making enough money so we've been talking about me getting a job outside the shop.'

Keith stared at her.

'That's right,' said Dad. 'Me and Mum don't like the idea, but the shop just isn't pulling in the trade, what with the new resort and the new snack bar in the pub.'

'We should have told you,' said Mum, 'but we were worried about how you'd feel because we know how much you like us working together.'

Suddenly Keith felt weak with relief. It was like having ninety kilos of ungutted cod lifted from his shoulders.

All the long faces and headaches and arguments and corrugated foreheads and droopy mouths hadn't been because anyone had stopped loving anyone.

They'd been because of a totally different problem.

A much easier one to solve.

Money.

FOUR

Keith put the coins into the slot and dialled.

'G'day,' said the wholesaler on the other end of the phone.

'This is Keith Shipley from the Paradise Fish Bar in Orchid Cove,' said Keith, 'and I'm in a phone box so I can't talk for long.'

'Do you want to place an order?' asked the wholesaler.

'No,' said Keith, 'I want to ask a favour.'

'I'm listening,' said the wholesaler.

'Well,' said Keith, 'our shop is operating in a pretty cut-throat business environment up here at the moment what with the new resort up the road and the new snack bar in the pub and it's really hard to make enough profit which is putting a serious strain on Mum and Dad, plus we're living in a small house with really thin walls so they can't even have sex that much so I was wondering if you could lower the price of your flour and oil a bit.'

There was a long pause at the other end.

'Is this a joke?' asked the wholesaler finally.

Don't be ridiculous, thought Keith. How could it be a joke? It's not even funny.

'It's an emergency,' said Keith, 'honest.'

'Look,' said the wholesaler, 'I'm operating in a pretty cut-throat business environment down here too. How would you like it if I rang you up at eight o'clock in the morning and went on about my financial problems?'

'You did,' said Keith. 'Last month.'

'Do your parents know you're doing this?' asked the wholesaler crossly.

'Sorry to bother you,' said Keith, and hung up.

He looked at the piece of paper with the phone numbers on it that he'd borrowed from the wall in the shop, and dialled again.

The potato distributor was even grumpier than the flour and oil wholesaler.

'Get nicked,' he said. 'Who do you think I am, Santa Claus?'

No chance of that, thought Keith, the only thing you've got in common with Santa Claus is a big bum.

He told the potato distributor that even a small price cut would help and that he himself had slashed his charge for peeling potatoes from five cents a potato to two cents, and the only reason he was charging Mum and Dad anything was that he had a car to repaint.

The potato wholesaler hung up.

Keith decided to try a different approach with the fish co-op.

At first it worked well.

Keith explained what he had in mind and the fish co-op man at the other end listened patiently even though Keith could hear people in the background yelling something about getting a move on and shifting some squid.

But when Keith had finished, the co-op man wasn't much help either. He explained that there wasn't any point in Keith getting up at three in the morning and coming down to the co-op with Tracy's dad's fish-gutting knife as all the fish were gutted on the boat. And anyway the co-op weren't allowed to give their fish-gutters cut-price fish as all the catch had to be sold at auction.

Keith asked if there was anything at the fish co-op that needed a paint job.

The man said 'fraid not.

Keith thanked him and hung up.

He felt panic bubbling up inside him.

It wasn't working.

Calm down, he told himself. Stop being a worry wart.

He took another deep breath.

It was time to tackle the problem face to face.

Keith found the pub owner in the bottle shop, hosing down the drive-through section.

'G'day young fella,' said the pub owner, hitching up his pyjama shorts, 'you've come to replace the compressor in my coolroom, have you?'

Keith remembered that the pub owner was famous throughout Orchid Cove for his sense of humour, which included putting blackcurrant syrup in blokes' beers when they weren't looking.

'I want to ask you a favour,' said Keith.

'Fire away,' said the pub owner.

Keith explained how it would really improve the quality of Mum and Dad's lives if the pub owner could leave fish and chips off the menu in his new snack bar and replace them with liver and onions, say, or rissoles.

The pub owner laughed so hard he hosed himself on the leg.

What's so funny? thought Keith. I didn't mention blackcurrant syrup.

'Nice try, young fella,' said the pub owner. 'If you're passing the new resort could you drop in and tell them how much they'd improve the quality of my life if they'd stop selling beer. Replace it with tea, say, or flavoured milk.'

He started laughing again.

As Keith walked away he noticed the girder with the off-white paint on it where Mum had hit it with the car door.

Keith wished she'd hit it harder.

The foyer of the new resort was as big as a football pitch and the carpet smelled like deodorant.

Keith walked over to the reception desk.

'Excuse me,' he said to a woman who was tapping the keys of a computer with fingernails that matched her Hot Sunflower jacket. 'Could I see the manager please?'

'The manager's not in till nine,' said the woman. 'What was it in connection with?'

Keith explained it was to do with the fish and chips on their menu.

'Bistro, coffee shop or the Coral Room?' she asked.

'All of them,' said Keith.

'We don't have fish and chips in the Coral Room,' she said, glancing at a menu. 'We have Reef Fillets And Deep-Fried Potato Skins In A Basket With Mango And Oyster Mayonnaise. Did you want to make a complaint?'

Keith explained that he didn't want to make a complaint, he was just wondering if the fish and chips could be taken off the menus. He explained about Mum and Dad's financial difficulties.

The receptionist said she'd pass his request on to the manager.

As he was leaving though, he glanced back and saw her pointing him out to a man with the same colour jacket and a ponytail.

They were both sniggering.

All right for them, thought Keith angrily. They obviously haven't got depressed parents to look after.

Keith stared out the classroom window and wished Mr Gerlach would talk a bit more quietly when a person was trying to think.

He looked down at the list he'd made on the last page of his exercise book.

Ways For A Fish Shop To Earn Extra Money
1. Charge for salt.
2. Sell steamed veggies (not broccoli).
3. Let people dry their washing over the fryer.
4. Raffle the really big potato scallops.

Keith sighed. It wasn't a lot for a morning's hard thinking.

He started to write down the idea he'd just had about letting kids have a go of the chip-cutting machine for five cents a turn. Then he stopped. Even if a hundred kids a week did it, which would totally disrupt Dad's chip-cutting routine, it would still only bring in five dollars and at least one of the kids was bound to lop off a finger which would cost more than that in medical bills and needles and cotton.

Keith sighed again.

There must be other ways to get rich in Australia.

Only last week in geography Ms O'Connell had been saying that Australia was a vast country full of natural resources. Iron ore was one she'd mentioned a lot.

Keith was in the middle of wondering whether the Health Department would let a fish shop sell iron ore when Mr Gerlach's voice burst into his thoughts.

'Keith Shipley,' said Mr Gerlach. 'Could you see your way clear to sparing us a bit of your attention when I'm talking about your work?'

Keith looked up.

Mr Gerlach was holding up a painting that Keith had done in art.

'As I was saying, Mr Shipley, your use of texture around the chin and neck here, giving a sort of warty, rough appearance to the skin, suggests the person is a man and quite an old one, am I right?'

'No, sir,' said Keith, 'it's a cane toad.'

The class howled with laughter.

'It is, sir,' said Keith indignantly.

Mr Gerlach glared the class into silence, then took several steps towards Keith.

'You were told,' said Mr Gerlach angrily, 'to do a painting of a face.'

'It's a cane toad's face,' said Keith quietly, wishing he'd done Gary Murdoch like he'd first planned to.

Mr Gerlach sighed loudly and stared out the window.

'Being a teacher,' he said, 'is like walking across Australia. It's lonely, it's hard going, and every day you stub your toe on exactly the same thing.'

He turned back and looked at the class.

'Lumps of rock.'

He looked out the window again.

'Sometimes you think you see something glittering and you stop and pick it up.'

He turned and looked at Keith.

'But it's just another lump of rock.'

He looked at the class.

'You'd think we teachers'd give up, wouldn't you?'

The class nodded.

'But we don't, do you know why?'

The class shook their heads.

'Because,' said Mr Gerlach, 'we dream that one day, somewhere in this great land of ours, we'll come across a precious stone.'

There was a pause while Mr Gerlach looked sadly

at Keith's painting and Keith felt excitement rushing through his veins.

'Excuse me, sir,' said Keith, 'What type of precious stone?'

FIVE

'Opal,' said Tracy's dad, leaning back on his chair on the verandah and swatting at a mosquito.

'See, dummy,' said Tracy, elbowing Keith in the ribs and almost knocking him off the old vinyl settee, 'told you there's no diamonds in Australia.'

'All right,' said Keith, 'it was just an idea.'

He tried not to show how bitterly disappointed he felt.

If Mr Gerlach had answered his simple question instead of making the whole class paint cane toads, he wouldn't have spent the whole afternoon getting excited about starting up a diamond mine and buying Mum and Dad a mansion with fountains and really thick bedroom walls.

'There are a few diamonds around,' said Tracy's dad, 'but they're as scarce as bubble baths in a drought. Opal's the go in Australia. Worth almost as much as diamonds and twice as good to look at.'

Keith sat forward on the settee.

This was what he wanted to hear.

'Have you got any?' he asked.

'Me?' laughed Tracy's dad. 'If I had any I wouldn't keep 'em sitting round the house. I'd sell 'em and get that flamin' suspension on the car fixed.'

'You rat,' said Tracy. 'You'd spend the money on that heap of rust when your own daughter's never even been to Brisbane. You mean poop.'

To Keith's amazement Tracy's dad didn't frown and stop Tracy's pocket money and send her to her room. He just grinned and threw a boot at Tracy. She ducked and grinned back at him.

I must remember, thought Keith, to ask Tracy why her parents are so cheerful. Perhaps they drink.

'I knew a bloke once,' said Tracy's dad, 'who was tearing across the scrub in his truck and he hit a boulder and bust an axle. He was ropeable. Miles from anywhere, crook truck, no money for repairs. He gave the boulder an almightly kick . . .'

Keith could see it, vivid in his imagination. He couldn't stop himself. 'And the boulder split open,' he said, 'and it was a huge opal.'

Tracy and her dad rocked with laughter.

Keith felt his cheeks go hot with embarrassment.

'You should take up writing for the telly,' said Tracy's dad, grinning at him. 'What I was going to say was he kicked the rock, started walking towards town, got a lift with a couple of blokes on their way to the opal fields, went there with them, and in the next week picked up ninety thousand dollars worth of opal.'

Keith's cheeks were still hot, but now it was with excitement.

'Where exactly are these opal fields?' he asked.

Keith and Tracy lay on Tracy's bedroom floor looking up at the map of Australia stuck to her ceiling.

'See all those little black oval shapes?' said Tracy. 'They show where the opal fields are.'

Keith squinted up. He could see white squiggles (sheep), brown handlebars (cattle) and grey possum poos (iron ore), but he couldn't see any black ovals.

Tracy reached under her bed and pulled out a fishing rod. She pointed up with it, touching the map.

'See,' she said. 'There's some.'

Keith squinted.

Tracy reached under the bed again and handed Keith a pair of binoculars.

He focussed them on the bit of the map she was pointing to.

Black ovals.

Opal fields.

And they weren't that far away from Orchid Cove. Only about the width of Tracy's light shade.

He was so busy picturing Mum and Dad's delighted faces when they heard the news that he didn't realize for ages that his shoulder was touching Tracy's.

'You gunna do your geography assignment about opal instead of iron ore?' asked Tracy. 'Ms O'Connell'd have kittens. Even more than Mr Gerlach had today.'

'No,' said Keith, 'I'm not. I probably won't even be doing the geography assignment at all.'

There was a silence.

Tracy swivelled her head and looked at him.

'Don't let it get you down,' she said quietly. 'If your mum and dad want to split up there's nothing you can do about it.'

Keith looked at her. I really like you, he thought, but you've got some weird ideas.

Keith ran up the front steps. At the door he stopped and took a deep breath. The tropical smells hit his nose like fruit salad and new shoes and pineapple sherbert lollies all at once.

And there was another smell, from inside the house. Spaghetti bolognese.

Nice one, thought Keith. Mum and Dad's favourite. Just the thing for them to be noshing while I tell them about our trip to the opal fields and the big house we'll be able to build up on the hill near Gary Murdoch's. With ninety-three taps. And six washers on each one. And a big verandah with a big table on it so we can sit around and tell jokes and laugh a lot.

Keith wondered if he should save the news till after dinner. People who broke into huge grins while they had mouths full of spaghetti bolognese tended to dribble down their fronts.

Won't matter, he thought. We'll have a washing machine soon.

He went in.

He couldn't hear the clatter of forks on plates, which meant they probably hadn't started. Dad would probably be at the sink doing the salad. Mum would probably be at the cupboard getting out the plates. The spaghetti bolognese would probably be on the table, steaming.

He'd tell them straight away and they'd turn to him, eyes shining through the steam.

He reached the kitchen.

And stopped.

Mum wasn't at the cupboard, she was standing gripping the fridge with both hands, face pale with anger, forehead criss-crossed with furrows.

Dad wasn't at the sink, he was standing with his back pressed against the window, face pale with shock, mouth drooping almost past his chin.

The spaghetti bolognese wasn't steaming on the table.

It was sliding down the wall next to Dad.

Keith looked at Mum again, then Dad, then the bolognese.

A cold lump was sliding down the inside of Keith's ribs at exactly the same speed as the meat sauce and bits of spaghetti were sliding down the wall.

Mum stepped forward and picked up the pot from the floor.

'Sorry love,' she said quietly to Keith. 'I lost my temper. I'll do you some sausages.'

'I'll do them,' said Dad.

Keith watched Mum and Dad avoid each other's eyes.

The sooner we're rich the better, he thought.

Keith told Mum and Dad about the opals after they'd all cleaned up the kitchen and had their sausages.

They listened carefully while he repeated Tracy's dad's truck story and explained how opals were almost as valuable as diamonds and told them that he'd checked the map and knew where to find some.

Dad turned the telly off.

They're not smiling, thought Keith. Perhaps it's shock. He'd seen a geezer in a film once who'd won the pools and had just turned grey and fainted into a rice pudding.

He was glad when Dad was safely sitting down again.

'Look Keith,' said Dad softly. 'We've got problems, I'm not denying that.'

'Financial problems,' said Mum.

'But,' said Dad, 'we're not going to solve them with crazy schemes.'

'You're a good kid,' said Mum, 'and we appreciate what you're trying to do, love, but Dad's right. Now come on, you've got school tomorrow, time to hit the sack. We'll talk about it some more in the morning.'

Even before Keith had left the room he knew it was pointless.

Some people just weren't capable of solving their own problems.

Some people had to have everything done for them.

Keith tapped softly on Tracy's window.

He listened.

All he could hear were the dawn cries of the birds in the forest at the back of Tracy's place.

He tapped again.

Suddenly there was a snuffling and snorting but it wasn't Tracy waking up, it was her dog Buster sniffing round Keith's school bag.

'Shhhh,' said Keith.

Buster looked as though he was about to bark.

Keith grabbed him round the mouth.

That's probably how you lost the leg and half the ear, thought Keith. Harassing friends of Tracy's who urgently need to speak to her.

Buster sneezed and Tracy opened her window.

She stared at Keith.

'Don't squeeze his mouth,' she said, 'he's got sore teeth.'

Once Keith was safely inside and Buster was in the corner contentedly chewing on Tracy's binoculars, Keith explained to Tracy that he needed to borrow a map showing how to get to the opal fields.

Tracy grinned. 'They agreed to go. Ripper.'

'No,' said Keith, 'they didn't. I'm going by myself.'

She looked at him.

Please, he thought, don't try and talk me out of it.

She didn't.

She stood on her bed and unstuck the map from the ceiling. Then she said three things that made Keith wish she was coming with him.

The first was that she wished she could go with him, but she'd promised her folks she'd never run away again after the time she'd tried to catch a bus to Melbourne when she was seven.

The second was how he'd need some extra money. She took all the notes and coins out of her cane toad money box and pressed them into his hand.

He started to say no, then remembered that all he had left of his own money was two dollars and eleven cents.

The third thing she whispered very close to his ear while she was holding the window up so he could climb out.

'Be careful you dopey mongrel.'

SIX

The first bit was easy.

Keith caught the early bus into Cairns along with an assortment of workers, backpackers and schoolkids.

The only dodgy moment was when he realized that the woman sitting two seats in front of him was Mrs Newman's grown-up daughter Gail.

Don't turn round, he thought.

It was the first telepathic message he'd sent for a while, but it worked.

She hobbled off the bus at Cairns Hospital without once glancing back.

Poor thing, thought Keith. When I've struck it rich I'll send her some money so she can take her family to live somewhere cooler where her feet won't swell up. That motel in Hobart perhaps.

At the bus station in Cairns things got more difficult.

Keith knew that any minute Mum and Dad would be waking up and going into his room and seeing his empty bed and finding his note.

And even though the note said not to worry because he'd be back soon with the opals and could they start talking to some builders, Keith was pretty sure they'd ring the police.

He had to move quickly.

Except there wasn't a bus that went all the way to the opal fields. Not the ones he wanted to go to, the ones Tracy had circled on the map, the ones where Tracy's dad's friend had struck it rich.

And even if he went as close as he could by bus, which wasn't very close, he'd use up nearly all his money on the ticket.

Keith stood back from the ticket window, desperately trying to think what to do.

If he started hitch-hiking this close to home the police would probably pick him up.

If he went to a bank and asked for a loan the bank manager would probably want to speak to Mum and Dad.

If he caught a taxi and offered the driver half the opals he was going to find, he'd probably have to hand over the other half to get back.

Then he saw it.

Across the road.

A big double-decker tourist bus with a crowd of tourists clambering aboard.

The destination window on the front of the bus said Brisbane, which meant it was going south.

It was a start.

Keith hurried across the road, waited until the driver had his head in the baggage compartment, then slipped aboard in the middle of a large family.

He went upstairs and sat near the front so he wouldn't look as though he was hiding.

Just as the bus was moving off, three women with white hair and T-shirts came upstairs and one of them sat next to him.

'Hey,' she said with an American accent, 'you just join the tour?'

Keith nodded.

Please, he thought, please don't be a retired FBI agent.

'Where are your folks?' asked the woman.

'Back there,' said Keith, pointing towards Orchid Cove.

No point in making up stories, she probably had a lie-detector machine in her overnight bag.

The woman glanced at the large family at the back of the bus and winked at Keith.

'More fun up the front, right?' she grinned. 'Hey, you should have been with us yesterday. We went to . . . what was it called?'

'Orchid Cove,' said her friend.

'Orchid Cove,' said the woman. 'A tropical paradise.'

Keith nodded politely. You wouldn't be saying that if you had your parents with you, he thought.

Then he noticed the plastic shopping bag the woman was holding on her lap.

Printed on it were the words *Ollie's Opals And Gifts, Duty Free Available.*

'Have you got any opals in there?' asked Keith.

'Sure have,' said the woman. 'Wanna peek?'

She rummaged in the bag, pulled out a wad of tissue paper, unfolded it and held up a thin metal chain.

Hanging from it, set in a clasp, was a small black stone.

'Twelve hundred dollars,' said the woman, 'but I got it for eleven hundred and fifty.'

As Keith stared, the bus jolted and the opal started to spin. Colours flashed from deep inside it. Tropical Parrot. Hot Sunflower. Charcoal Red. Pacific Blue. Frothy Orange. Dusky Pink. Vatican Purple.

Blimey, thought Keith, I've seen whole colour charts that haven't had this many colours in them.

And he'd never seen colours so bright, not even on picnics when he closed his eyes in the sun and pressed bread rolls into his eye sockets.

Later, after the woman had dozed off, Keith stared out the bus window and thought about how many opals he'd be able to fit into his school bag.

A million dollars worth at least.

Suddenly even the colours of the trees and houses and glimpses of ocean flashing past seemed brighter.

The bus slowed down as it went through a town and Keith, wrestling with Tracy's map, realized it was the town where he had to get off to go inland to the opal fields.

He folded the map frantically.

How could he stop a bus without drawing attention to himself?

Even as he was trying to choose between telepathy and nudging the sleeping American woman so she slumped on to the emergency buzzer, he saw that they were passing a road junction.

His turn-off.

He jumped to his feet.

He'd just have to go down and tell the driver that he was sorry but he'd got on the wrong bus after receiving a blow to the head playing softball.

Then the bus pulled into a service station.

Amazing, thought Keith. I've just stopped a bus with telepathy and I didn't even know I was doing it.

'Morning tea,' said the American woman's friend.

'Look at you,' said the American woman to Keith. 'On your feet already. You must have done this trip before.'

Keith grabbed his school bag and hurried back to the stairs and stepped into the middle of the large family and clattered down with them and off the bus.

He realized he was shaking.

With luck like this, he thought, when I get to the opal field I might have to buy a second school bag.

In the service station cafe Keith bought two postcards and went into the toilets and locked himself in a cubicle.

While he waited for the bus to leave he wrote the postcards.

Dear Mum and Dad,

This is just to let you know that I took the torch, the hammer, the gardening trowel, the plastic strainer, the chocolate biscuits, and the stuff that's missing from the bathroom and my clothes drawer. So it's OK, you haven't been burgled. I'm fit and well. Please don't worry, things are looking even better than I thought opal-wise.

Love, Keith.

Dear Tracy,
Wish you were here.
Keith.
PS. IOU $24.35.
(signed) Keith Shipley.
PPS. Thanks.

Then he ate four chocolate biscuits.

At last he heard the bus revving away into the distance.

He went back into the café for a milkshake. The mid-morning news was just starting on a TV on the wall.

Keith froze.

What if there was a nationwide alert out for him and his photo appeared on the screen?

There might even be a reward.

The other customers would jump him.

He wouldn't stand a chance.

And he'd just ordered a milkshake so he couldn't leave without looking obvious.

Keith stared at the screen, holding his breath.

The Prime Minister in Canberra.

Floods in Bangladesh.

Cockatoos playing chess in Gympie.

Then it was over.

Keith sat down for a minute and let relief and milk-shake flood through him.

Funny though, he thought, that there isn't a nation-wide search yet. Police must be double checking that Mum and Dad aren't loonies.

Keith finished his milkshake and started walking back towards the road junction.

One good thing about the police not looking for him yet, he could hitch a lift. And in a friendly country like Australia he'd get one in no time.

Keith put on his friendliest face as the car turned off the highway and headed towards him.

He stuck out his hand with his thumb pointing towards the opal fields and tried to look like someone who was not only great at conversation but didn't make smells in cars.

The car roared past.

Keith closed his eyes as the dust billowed around him.

He felt dizzy and weak.

He looked at his watch, squinting in the glare of the sun.

Nearly four hours he'd been standing there.

Eighteen vehicles.

What was the matter with people? He didn't look like a murderer or a terrorist.

He rubbed some more sun-block cream on his face and adjusted the knotted T-shirt on his head.

If he didn't have something to eat or drink soon the nineteenth vehicle would be an ambulance.

He picked up his school bag and plodded slowly back towards the service station.

It was the most beautiful sight he'd seen since arriving in Australia, including Orchid Cove beach at sunset and mango ice-cream.

It was parked next to the service station café and Keith felt like running over and kissing it.

He didn't because if you were trying to keep a low profile it was best not to be seen kissing a semi-trailer with a bulldozer on the back.

It wasn't the battered truck itself that made Keith's spirits pick themselves up and do a little dance, or the dust-covered bulldozer. It was the South Australian number plates.

If the truck was heading home it would be going inland, south-west, through the opal fields.

Keith went into the cafe.

He held his breath.

Nobody jumped on him and yelled for a reward, so the nationwide search obviously still hadn't started.

He asked the man behind the counter if he knew who was driving the truck with the bulldozer on the back.

'I am,' said a voice.

Keith turned.

The truck driver, a big man with earrings, was eating sausages and eggs and watching *Play School* on TV.

'Are you going inland towards South Australia?' asked Keith.

'Yep,' said the truck driver.

'Could I have a lift please?' asked Keith.

'Nope,' said the truck driver.

There was a long pause filled only by the sound of Big Ted building a suspension bridge out of cornflakes packets.

'Company policy,' said the truck driver. 'No lifts.'

'Anyway,' said the man behind the counter, 'aren't you a bit young? Where's your parents.'

'Back there,' said Keith, pointing towards Orchid Cove.

He hurried outside.

I bet if you read that company policy carefully, thought Keith, it says no lifts *in* the truck, not no lifts *on* the truck.

He looked around.

No one was watching.

He climbed on to the back of the truck, opened the bulldozer cabin door, crawled in, closed the door, and lay on the cabin floor hugging his school bag.

Keith lay there, by his calculation, through the rest of *Play School*, all of *Danger Mouse*, and some of *Gumby*.

Then the truck door slammed and the engine roared and they started to move.

Keith tried to make himself as small as he could. He pressed his cheek to the metal floor and the vibrations through his cheekbone made him see stars.

He closed his eyes and imagined each exploding point of light was an opal.

SEVEN

'All right you – out.'

Keith sat up, cold and dazed and aching.

Something was different.

The vibrations had stopped.

So had his dream. He'd been on a yacht with Mum and Dad, a luxury yacht with built-in fish fryers and solid opal taps.

The man with the earrings and the scowl hadn't been on the yacht.

He was here now though, glaring at Keith.

'I said no lifts,' growled the man.

For a moment Keith wondered if the man was a lift operator, then remembered he was a truck driver.

A pang of fear gripped Keith just before the truck driver did.

Keith grabbed his school bag as the truck driver dragged him out of the bulldozer and down off the back of the truck.

He staggered and blinked. The sun was just coming up over the horizon.

'Where are we?' asked Keith as his teeth started to chatter.

'Twelve hours inland,' said the truck driver. 'Which means it'll take you about twelve weeks to walk back.'

Keith looked around. It was the country all right, but there weren't any trees, just bushes and dry grass.

And concrete. He was standing on a square of concrete with two petrol pumps on it, and a small fibro office to one side.

'Is this the opal fields?' asked Keith, struggling to control his teeth.

'Opal fields?' said the truck driver, with a snort of laughter. 'They're four hours further on. If you start now you should get there in four weeks.'

'Leave him alone, Col,' said a voice.

Keith turned and saw another man with a plump face and dirty orange overalls coming over from the office.

'He's only a kid,' said the other man.

'Still could have got me the sack,' said Col.

'Get lost,' said the other man. 'When was the last time you saw an inspector out here?'

'Could happen,' muttered Col.

The other man turned to Keith.

'You on your own?' he asked.

Keith took a deep breath, sent his teeth a stern telepathic message, and told the two men about Mum and Dad's financial problems.

Col leant against the truck and rubbed his face in his hands and listened gravely.

The other man looked at Keith and then at the ground and then back at Keith.

They're sympathetic, thought Keith. They can see I can't afford to waste time and they're going to help me.

He'd just finished thinking that when they took him across and locked him in the office.

Keith sat in a cracked vinyl swivel chair and stared gloomily at a model train on a shelf on the office wall.

Outside he could hear Col and the other man arguing about him.

'It'd only be till tonight, Mick, the cops'd be here before dark,' said Col.

'You can't leave him here,' said Mick. 'I'm not having the cops coming out here. I've got an unregistered tow truck out the back and six microwaves I'm looking after for someone.'

'Well I can't take him to the cops,' said Col, 'not with the state of my log-book.'

Keith wondered what the wages would be like in prison. Probably take twenty years to earn enough for a yacht.

He wondered if Tracy would come and visit him.

He wondered what she'd say if she was here now.

'Jeez, you're a worry wart,' that's what she'd say.

Suddenly he knew what he had to do.

He went and banged on the office door as loudly as he could.

'Col, Mick,' he shouted. 'Open up a sec.'

The door flew open and the two men stood there, looking at him.

'Col,' said Keith, 'if you take me to the opal fields I'll paint your truck.'

Col stared at him.

'And the bulldozer too if you want,' said Keith. 'I'm

good at it, I've done a car and a fish and chip shop.'

Col and Mick exchanged a glance.

Col sighed.

Mick grinned.

Col stared at the horizon and rubbed the back of his neck for about a minute.

'All right,' said Col, 'paint my truck and if it's any good I'll take you as far as the opal fields.'

'Thanks,' said Keith, 'you won't regret it.'

'Get him some paint, Mick,' said Col.

Keith went over and walked round the truck. It was at least twelve times bigger than the Corolla.

This could take all day, he thought. Hope they've got a big brush.

Mick came over and handed Keith a cardboard box.

Inside were some tiny tins of hobby paint and some skinny little brushes.

Keith stared at them.

'I build model trains,' said Mick sheepishly.

Keith looked up at the truck towering over him.

That's all I need, he thought. Stranded in the bush with a couple of loonies.

'I won't get half a bumper bar done with these,' he said. He spoke softly so as not to startle Mick and cause him to have a fit or a violent outburst or something.

Col appeared and handed Keith a piece of plywood.

'There you go,' he said, 'you can do it on that.' He went and stood next to the truck. 'Is this a good place for me to stand?'

Suddenly Keith understood.

Col didn't want him to paint the truck, he wanted him to paint a picture of the truck.

Mick brought a wooden crate for Keith to sit on, which was just as well because Keith's knees had suddenly gone a bit wobbly.

It wasn't that Keith didn't like painting pictures, he did.

But every time he painted one something seemed to go wrong.

At school Mr Gerlach had kittens.

At home Mum and Dad got tense and unhappy just because a couple of times Keith had left tubes of paint on the settee with the tops off and Dad had sat on them.

OK, said Keith to himself, stop being a worry wart. Mr Gerlach isn't here. Mum and Dad aren't here. There's just me and Mick in the office and Col standing over there sticking his chest out.

'Behind the wheel might be better,' Keith told Col.

Col climbed up into the cab.

Keith picked up a stub of a pencil and started sketching the truck on to the plywood.

He'd be OK as long as it didn't end up looking like a cane toad.

'Finished yet?' called Col. 'My arms have gone numb.'

'Nearly,' said Keith. 'Hang on.'

Just a few more dabs of Burnt Ochre on Col's cowboy hat and . . .

'OK,' said Keith, 'finished.'

Col climbed stiffly down from the cab, rubbing his arms, and looked at the painting.

Keith crossed his fingers and hoped Col's mum and dad had taken him to lots of art galleries when he was a kid.

If he likes the colour of the truck, thought Keith, I'm probably OK.

It had been a big risk, changing the colour of the truck to purple, but off-white wouldn't have shown up as well against the gold and silver sunrise. He'd thought at first of making the truck orange, but that would have clashed with the blue snake wrapped around the black bulldozer.

If he likes the snake, thought Keith, I'm probably OK.

He peeped up at Col's face.

Col was frowning.

'It's flying,' he said. 'The truck's flying.'

'That's right,' said Keith. 'I've painted it from the point of view of a truck inspector as you roar out of the sunrise over his head.'

'What are those things flying around the truck?' asked Col.

'Vampire bats,' said Keith.

'What's that gleam coming from Col's mouth?' asked Mick, who'd come over from the office.

'An opal tooth,' said Keith.

Col slowly broke into a grin.

'It's a beauty,' he said to Keith. 'Let's go.'

He gave Keith a leg-up into the cab, said hooroo to Mick, gunned the motor and they were off.

While they bounced along the dusty road Keith told Col about South London and how big trucks from Europe used to get wedged under the pub overhang coming round the corner from Pontifract Road.

Col told Keith about the Birdsville Track and how once he'd hit a pot-hole so big he'd lost three hundred fan heaters and the can of drink he was holding at the time.

Then the vibrations from the road started to make Keith feel drowsy and he closed his eyes and thought about the opal fields and wondered if they really were fields or if they were just called that because the glittering opals were in rows like strawberries.

EIGHT

Keith snapped awake.

Col was leaning across him, pushing open the door of the cab.

'Is this the opal fields?' croaked Keith, squinting through the dusty windscreen.

'Yep,' said Col.

All Keith could see was dust.

The only things glinting were Col's eyes as he looked up at Keith's painting, which he'd stuck to the roof of the cab with muffler tape.

'She's a ripper,' he said. 'Blokes at the depot'll chuck their guts when they see it.'

'Thanks,' said Keith.

He grabbed his school bag and jumped down from the cab.

The heat hit him in the face like Mr Gerlach's breath after a curry lunch.

'Don't forget,' said Col, 'if the cops pick you up, leave me out of it.'

'OK,' said Keith.

Col gunned the motor and the truck started to move off.

'And give your folks a ring,' he yelled.

'I'm going to,' shouted Keith, waving.

And I am, he thought, as he watched the truck disappear down the dirt road, just as soon as I've got the opals.

He looked at the ground around him.

It certainly wasn't a field. More a piece of desert with tyre tracks and a few wispy bits of dry grass.

And no opals to be seen.

They must be in the dust.

He dropped to his knees, opened his school bag, and felt around in the thick orange powder.

Nothing.

Just dust.

Then he touched something small and round and hard.

He picked it up and blew the dust off it.

It sparkled.

Heart pounding, he rubbed it on his jeans.

This one opal, he thought, could pay for the plumbing in our new house, or a month's holiday for Mum and Dad in a balloon, or a fishing boat so we can catch our own fish, or a Rolls Royce with speed stripes, or a . . .

The opal had stopped sparkling.

Keith saw why.

It had been wrapped in silver paper, which Keith had shredded with his rubbing.

And it wasn't an opal at all, it was a piece of old bubblegum.

Keith tossed it away.

OK, he said to himself, be sensible. You're not

going to find opals lying here by the side of the road. Any opals here would have been picked up years ago by people driving to the shops who remembered they'd left their money at home and needed a couple of precious stones to pay for the groceries.

Keith stood up and looked around.

Now the dust from the truck had settled, he could see he was in the middle of a vast, flat plain with hardly anything sprouting out of it.

Anything green, that is.

There were other things, brown things, most of them taller than Keith, dotted over the landscape for as far as he could see.

Piles of dirt.

Keith had a horrible suspicion he knew what they were.

Keith decided to check out the town first and buy some cans of drink because he'd seen a movie once where some prospectors had run out of water in the desert and had got dehydrated and started seeing piles of gold that were really donkeys.

All he could see were two buildings and a caravan park.

'Excuse me,' he said to a man climbing into a four wheel drive, 'where's the town?'

The man grinned and knocked some dust out of his beard with his hat.

'You're standing in it,' he said.

Keith looked at the buildings.

One was a pub with cement brick walls and a corrugated iron roof and a wooden verandah and a huge dirt car-park.

The other was a shop with fibro walls and a corrugated iron roof and a wooden verandah and a huge dirt car-park.

Over the shop door was a sign saying *Curly's Store*.

I hope Curly sells cold drinks, thought Keith as he went in.

When his eyes got used to the gloom, he saw that Curly sold everything. Food, hardware, clothes, make-up, camping gear, kitchen utensils, dog care products, and that was just on the first shelf Keith looked at.

Curly also sold newspapers.

Keith held his breath while he checked to see if any of the headlines said NATIONWIDE SEARCH FOR BRAVE OPAL BOY.

They didn't.

Keith felt relieved, but with a twinge of disappointment. Then he saw that the papers were three days old.

'Can I help you?' said a gruff voice.

Standing behind the counter was an elderly man wearing an off-white T-shirt with *Curly* printed on it. He was completely bald.

That's a bit rough, thought Keith, giving a person a nickname just cause he's got hairy arms.

Keith bought three cans of drink and a meatloaf sandwich. Once the sandwich was in his mouth he realized how ravenous he was and bought two more.

Then he got down to business.

'Those piles of dirt,' asked Keith, 'are they . . . ?'

'Mullock dumps,' said Curly, slapping a piece of meatloaf on to a piece of bread, 'from the diggings.'

'How long does it take to dig an opal mine?' asked Keith, dreading the answer.

'If you've got a diesel drill and some gelignite,' said Curly, 'you can get a decent shaft down in a day. By hand it takes weeks.'

Keith felt a lump in his stomach that wasn't meatloaf.

'You don't happen to know of any spare mines around here, do you?' he asked. 'Ones where the owners have struck it rich and gone to Disneyland.'

Curly gave Keith a look that made him think Curly must have once had a bad experience at Disneyland.

'We've got a rule out here,' said Curly. 'You never touch another bloke's mine. Never.'

'What happens if you do?' asked Keith in a small voice, hoping he sounded like he was doing this for a school project.

Curly reached under the counter.

Keith wondered if he was going to produce a school project kit.

But it wasn't a cardboard folder that Curly thumped down on to the counter.

It was a big, black, double-barrelled shotgun.

Keith stood on the store verandah, swallowed his last bit of meatloaf sandwich, and looked around for a good place to fossick.

When Curly had first mentioned the word fossick,

Keith had feared it was a technical term meaning to dig up opals with a bulldozer and a dump truck.

Then Curly had explained that it simply meant picking up opals by hand on the surface rather than digging down for them, and that just as many opals were found by fossickers as by the crazies who sank shafts half way to Belgium.

Keith spotted a good place to fossick.

Keith looked at his watch and sighed.

Ten forty-three.

He'd been on his hands and knees in the pub car-park for twenty-five minutes in the scorching sun and all he'd found, apart from a few thousand stones and rocks and a few hundred cigarette butts and beer bottle tops, was a bleached bone from a small animal or lizard.

He sighed again.

When opal miners got drunk and spun their tyres, they obviously jumped out of the car afterwards to check for opals.

He looked at his watch again.

Ten forty-four.

He'd planned to find all the opals he needed by twelve-thirty so he could organise a charter plane to get him back to Orchid Cove in time for dinner.

He looked at the bleached bone again.

Maybe it wasn't part of a lizard.

Maybe it was part of a barbecued chicken.

Or a fossicker.

Keith decided to try somewhere else.

*

Keith looked at his watch and sighed.

Eleven twenty-seven.

He'd been on his hands and knees in the caravan park for thirty-eight minutes in the scorching sun and all he'd found was a shoelace and a plastic hose nozzle.

It wasn't much of a caravan park, just a square of dust with a dozen or so battered caravans, but he'd hoped the van wheels might have stirred up the odd gem or two.

Nothing.

A voice broke into his thoughts.

'Scuse me.'

It belonged to a middle-aged woman in a fluffy dressing-gown.

Keith thought she must be melting. He was wearing a T-shirt and he felt like a chip in oil.

'While you're down there, love,' she said, 'could you do me a favour? Keep an eye out for a filling. Merv threw up on his way back from the pub last night and lost one.'

Keith said that normally he'd be happy to, but he'd just decided to try somewhere else.

Keith looked at his watch.

He didn't have the energy to sigh.

Nineteen minutes past twelve.

He'd been on his hands and knees by the petrol pumps at the side of Curly's store for nearly an hour in the scorching sun and all he'd found was a tyre valve and three pieces of old bubblegum.

So much for his theory that when truck drivers stopped for diesel and jumped down from their cabs, the heels of their cowboy boots would gouge out opals.

Keith pulled the knotted T-shirt off his head and wiped the dust and sweat off his face.

This is hopeless, he thought.

Not just this spot, the whole trip.

Coming all this way had been a stupid waste of time, thirty-two hours of worry and discomfort and knots in the guts, all for nothing.

The only good bit had been painting Col's truck.

Keith looked round for a phone box so he could ring Mum and Dad and tell them he was coming home as soon as a truck came past that would swap him a lift for a painting.

He had a vision of Mum and Dad's faces glowing with relief at his safe return.

Then he saw the disappointment gradually furrowing Mum's forehead and drooping Dad's mouth as they realized he hadn't brought any opals.

Disappointment closely followed by migraines and upset tummies and crosswords and solitary bush walks and arguments and . . .

Keith stood up and went into the store.

NINE

'Noodling,' said Curly, slapping a piece of meatloaf on to a piece of bread.

Keith lowered his lemonade and stared at him.

Noodling?

What did spaghetti have to do with finding opals?

'Sifting through the mullock dumps,' said Curly. 'Picking up bits of colour the shafties have missed. Best way to fossick.'

Of course, thought Keith, his body suddenly tingling and not just from the lemonade or the sunburn. That's where I've been going wrong. No noodling.

'One important thing to remember when you choose a dump,' said Curly, handing him the sandwich. 'If there's someone working the shaft, make sure you ask their permission. And even if a shaft looks deserted, don't go down it.'

'Don't worry,' said Keith through a mouthful of meatloaf, 'I won't.'

What was the point of going down a mine, finding opals worth hundreds of thousands of dollars and then spending most of it on having shotgun pellets surgically removed?

'You won't find big stuff like this in the mullocks,' said Curly, thumping a big dirty rock on to the counter, 'but you might pick up some of these.' He rattled a jam jar half full of tiny dirty rocks.

Keith stared at the dirty rocks to make sure he wasn't seeing things.

Yes, they were definitely dirty rocks.

So that's why Curly was called Curly. It wasn't his arm-hairs, it was his brain.

'Thanks for the advice,' said Keith, backing towards the door, 'and they're great-looking rocks, but I've only got room in my bag for opals.'

Curly grinned for the first time since Keith had met him.

Oh no, thought Keith, here's where he grabs his shotgun and runs amok.

But instead Curly rubbed some of the dirt off the big rock and held it up in front of a window. Colours flashed out of it.

'Never looks much till it's cut and polished,' said Curly.

Keith went over and took the rock from him and ran his fingers over the rough sandstone and the smooth ribbons of flashing opal running through it.

Suddenly he didn't feel exhausted any more.

He couldn't wait to get out on the mullock dumps and start sifting through the dirty rocks and sorting out which ones were opals.

'Thanks very much,' he said to Curly, handing him the rock. 'You've made a troubled family very happy.'

He headed for the door.

'Just a sec,' said Curly. 'Talking about families, where's yours?'

Keith froze.

He forced his mouth open to tell Curly the story he'd made up earlier that morning, the one about Mum and Dad being kidnapped by Taiwanese pirates who were demanding a ransom of opals and potato scallops, but suddenly it didn't seem like such a good story.

He tried to make up another one, but his brain had turned to dust.

Helplessly he pointed in what he thought was the direction of Orchid Cove.

'Good-o,' said Curly, 'they're in the caravan park. Just checking they're not camped on my claim.'

Keith looked at his watch and sighed.

Two thirty-three.

He'd been squatting on this mullock heap with the scorching wind blowing dust into his eyes and mouth for over an hour and a half.

He must have sifted tonnes of dirt through Mum's plastic strainer.

He'd smashed hundreds of dirty rocks with Dad's hammer.

Nothing.

He looked across at the next heap where an Aboriginal family were systematically sifting the dirt and chatting and laughing.

'How ya goin?' one of the women called across to him.

'Not very well,' Keith shouted back.

'Don't give up,' yelled the woman, 'we found heaps in there last week.'

*

Keith looked at his watch and coughed.

Twenty past four.

This second dump was no better. He must have sifted just about the whole thing, most of it in the plastic strainer and the rest in his mouth, and he hadn't found a single opal.

Plus there was the whine.

The opal fields were noisy enough, with generators and drills clattering away, but coming from behind the next dump was a high-pitched whine that made concentrating on finding opals impossible.

Keith couldn't stand it any longer.

He threw down his trowel and strainer and stormed over the next dump towards the whine.

As soon as he got over the top he saw what it was.

A small generator strapped to a tent on legs.

Keith went over and tapped the tent on the shoulder.

A flap opened and a man's face, eerily lit by a purple light, peered out.

'Excuse me, but do you have to make so much noise?' said Keith.

'Sorry,' said the man. 'Ultraviolet light. Shows up the opal.'

'Have you found any?' asked Keith.

'Absolutely,' said the man. 'Last week.'

'Well it's nice to know there's some around,' said Keith. 'I'd just about given up on that heap over there.'

'You won't find any over there,' said the man.

'Why not?' asked Keith.

'Because,' said the man, 'I did that yesterday.'

Keith dropped his school bag and wiped the sweat off his face.

At last he'd found one.

A mullock heap that hadn't been noodled in the last week.

In fact this one had wisps of dry grass growing on it so perhaps it had never been noodled at all.

Fat chance.

But he had to keep trying.

There was an old caravan by the dump so Keith banged on the door and called out to see if anyone was home.

No one was.

He went over to the shaft and yelled down it.

No one answered.

Then he noticed the sign.

Keep Out. Private Claim. By Order Of C. Kovacs, General Store.

Blimey, thought Keith, this must be Curly's mine.

Then another thought came to him. With Curly back at the store, this was his chance to check out an opal mine without getting shot.

He shone his torch down the shaft, but couldn't even see the bottom.

Keith knew he had to go down.

Just for a look.

Above the shaft was a winch with a coil of thick

wire. Keith uncoiled the wire and it slithered down into the darkness.

When it went slack he knew it had touched the bottom. He put the torch in his mouth, gripped the wire with both hands, planted the soles of his feet against the sides of the shaft and half climbed, half slid down in a shower of dirt and rock fragments.

The bottom of the shaft was cool and dark.

He shone the torch around. There was a tunnel running off to one side, high enough to walk along.

Keith didn't.

He gazed for a while at the walls of the tunnel, at the bands and seams of rock running along it. Some looked hard, some looked crumbly, and any one of them could have been stuffed with opal.

But he didn't touch.

He didn't want to be a thief.

He wanted to be a miner.

Curly stared at Keith, the lump of meatloaf and the slice of bread in his hands forgotten.

'Paint my store?'

'That's right,' said Keith. 'I'll paint your store in return for a day down your mine. As long as I can keep everything I find down there.'

Curly thought about this for a long time.

'There's not much down there,' he said. 'I've given up on it.'

Oh yeah, thought Keith, so why have you got a big Keep Out sign plastered all over it?

'I'll pay for the paint,' said Keith.

He'd already seen a paintbox for eleven dollars fifty on the stationery shelf and a big drawing pad for three dollars.

That was nearly all the money he had left but it was worth it.

'Are you any good?' asked Curly.

'I did a truck on the way here and the owner was delighted,' said Keith.

Curly thought some more.

'OK,' he said, 'it's a deal. Paint this place and you can have full use of my claim for twenty-four hours.'

They shook hands.

'I'll do it tomorrow,' said Keith.

'You'd better buy the paint now,' said Curly, 'because I'm away on business most of tomorrow.'

Keith went to the stationery shelf and grabbed the paintbox and pad.

When he got back to the counter he saw that Curly was over at the other side of the store doing a sum on his fingers.

'I reckon,' said Curly, 'you'll need about twenty litres to do the outside of this place. That'll be a hundred and eighty-five dollars please.'

TEN

The first half-litre was the hardest.

Keith knocked on the door of the first caravan and a man in off-white underpants appeared. He looked like he'd just woken up.

'Sorry to disturb you so early,' said Keith, 'but have you got any old paint to spare? I'm painting Curly's store.'

The man stared at him.

'Not a picture,' Keith added, 'the store itself.' He thought he'd better get that straight as it could be a bit confusing.

'Why doesn't Curly supply the paint?' growled the man.

'He's supplying the step-ladder and the dust sheets,' said Keith, 'and I'm supplying the paint.'

'Why?' growled the man.

'It's a long story,' said Keith, 'but it involves raising money for a very worthy cause.'

'What worthy cause?' growled the man.

'Well,' said Keith, 'my mum and dad have got this fish and chip shop way over on the coast and the hotel has just started up a snack bar and the new resort round on the headland has got three restaurants and . . .'

'Hang on,' grunted the man.

He went inside the van and Keith heard him clattering about. He came back with a litre tin of paint, handed it to Keith and closed the door.

'Thanks,' Keith called out.

He opened the tin with the claw end of Dad's hammer. The tin was half full of dull red anti-rust paint.

Nice one, thought Keith. Only nineteen-and-a-half litres to go.

The door of the second caravan swung open and the middle-aged woman in the fluffy dressing-gown smiled at Keith.

'It's O K, love,' she said, 'we found it. I superglued it back in and he's eaten steak on it and everything.'

Keith explained that he hadn't come about the filling, he'd come about paint.

'Merv,' she called into the van, 'dig out that aquamarine gloss.' She turned back to Keith. 'We got it to do the van but it was too bright. Good for a shop, though. Excuse me asking, but what are those lines on your face?'

For a moment Keith didn't know what she was talking about. Then he realized.

'It was the sheet,' he explained. 'When I was asleep last night. It got scrunched up under my face.'

He didn't explain that it had been a dust sheet. Or that it had got scrunched up because he'd been tense all night in case Curly had come by and found him sleeping on the store verandah and called the cops.

The woman's husband appeared with a four litre

paint can and the woman insisted on opening his mouth and showing Keith the filling. Keith didn't mind because the can was two-thirds full.

The next four vans didn't have any paint, but then Keith hit the jackpot.

A youngish bloke with tattoos stuck his head out of his caravan window and grinned when he heard what Keith was doing.

'Your lucky day, mate,' he said.

He told Keith how he'd been employed by the Department of Main Roads to paint the white posts by the side of the highway and how he'd painted them all the way to the opal fields and then had got bored and chucked it in.

'Do you need any brushes or turps?' he asked as he pulled the tarpaulin off the back of his van.

'No thanks,' said Keith, wishing he hadn't spent all his money except eleven cents buying brushes and turps from Curly.

The bloke swung a ten litre drum off the back of the van.

'It's white,' he said, 'with reflective particles.'

Keith couldn't believe his luck.

He thanked the bloke and said he hoped the bloke found enough opals to pay someone else to paint the white posts. Then he started rolling the drum towards the store.

After a bit he stopped.

A news bulletin was just beginning on a radio in one of the vans.

Keith listened carefully, but there was no mention of any nationwide searches.

Keith wondered why not.

Perhaps Mum and Dad hadn't gone to the police.

Perhaps they didn't want to find him.

Perhaps they were glad he'd gone.

He pushed the thoughts out of his mind.

He was much too busy to be a worry wart.

By the time Keith was halfway round the diggings, word had spread that he was doing up Curly's place and people gave him paint without even being asked.

Two kids from the Aboriginal family Keith had met the day before ran up and gave him a half tin of Royal Purple and a full tin of Mandarin Orange, which, they explained, were unwanted Christmas presents.

The ultraviolet man popped out of his corrugated iron hut and handed over a quarter litre of matt black left over from painting the metal detector he'd been using before he got his ultraviolet machine.

A man with a beard and a European accent rode up on a motor bike and tossed Keith nearly two litres of Signal Red. He said he'd been using it to paint signs around his shaft saying *Tresspassers Will Be Stabbed* but he didn't need it now because he'd become a Jehovah's Witness.

Even as Keith was thanking the man for the paint and the pamphlets, he saw the sun glinting off yet more tins as people carried them towards him across the mullock heaps.

*

Keith crouched in front of the store, picked up Dad's hammer and levered the lids off the twenty-seven tins of paint and gave them all a good stir except the four that had gone solid.

By his calculation he had eighteen and a half litres.

It'll be enough, he told himself. When Curly said twenty he probably thought I'd be slapping it on like an amateur. He didn't know I already had a fish and chip shop and a Toyota Corolla under my belt.

Keith poured the Royal Purple into the Department of Main Roads Reflective White and stirred until he had a pastel violet that was just like the Autumn Crocus on the golf buggies at the Orchid Cove Resort.

He looked at his watch.

Nine forty-three.

The woman in the pub had said that Curly usually got back from his card game on Sundays at about six.

Eight hours and seventeen minutes left.

Time to start painting.

Keith didn't look at his watch.

His neck and back and arms were aching too much to make the effort, plus there was no point as his watch was covered with a big dollop of Mongolian Beige.

He needed all his strength to keep painting and not fall off the step-ladder.

He finished the Celery Green section of the guttering and grinned wearily as the applause broke out again.

It had been like this for a couple of hours now. Every time he used up a colour the crowd that had gathered to watch would give him a clap.

That's probably what's kept me going, he thought, as he forced his wobbly legs down the step-ladder. That and the food and drink. If he'd eaten everything they'd offered him he'd have exploded and Curly's store would have been even more multicoloured than it was now.

Three verandah posts to go and he was finished.

Keith washed the brush in turps and dipped it into the Poinsettia Masonry Acrylic.

He heard a truck pull up and turned anxiously, hoping it wasn't Curly.

It was the young bloke with tattoos.

'Do you want a hand?' he yelled.

'Rack off Gibbo,' said someone in the crowd. 'This is art.'

Keith grinned again.

It wasn't just mates who knew how to say the right thing.

Then, after Keith had finished the verandah posts and was giving the door another coat to use up the Flaming Pink, he heard another truck pull up, this time with a long skid and a crunch as it ran into a parked truck.

Keith watched Curly climb out of the van.

Curly looked dazed.

Not by the accident, by what he was seeing.

Keith watched as Curly took in the Mongolian Beige roof, the Aquamarine, Morning Mist, Velvet Moss and Celery Green guttering, the Matt Black down-pipes, the Autumn Crocus walls, the Vivid Coral window frames (that was inspired although I say it myself, thought Keith, mixing the Signal Red and Mandarin Orange like that), the Flaming Pink door with the Dull Red Anti-Rust handle, and the Corfu Blue, Autumn Yellow, Pale Eggplant, Grecian Dusk and Poinsettia verandah posts.

Keith held his breath.

Curly's mouth hung open.

Then the crowd broke into cheers and applause and slapped Curly on the back and told him he had the only general store in Central Queensland that was not only a major tourist attraction but could also be used by aircraft for navigating in heavy fog.

Bit by bit Curly's face relaxed into a grin and soon he was inviting everyone in for cold drinks on the house.

On the way in he shook Keith's hand and asked Keith to autograph the bottom of the wall.

Keith proudly painted his signature with the last of the matt black and said he'd be in for a drink in a sec but first he had to do a bit of guttering he'd missed.

He forced his rubbery legs back up the step-ladder.

As he smoothed on the last brushfuls of Morning Mist he looked across the roof at the vast plain that stretched away to the horizon.

Suddenly the inside of his chest felt vast as well.

With happiness.

And the feeling didn't go away when he realized he was having it. It stayed there right up to the moment when he finished off the piece of guttering and was just about to climb down the step-ladder and saw, in the distance, coming towards him along the dirt road, getting bigger by the second, the Tropical Parrot Corolla with the Hot Sunflower speed stripes.

ELEVEN

I'm a worry wart, thought Keith.

I must be.

I'm standing here with a knot in my guts when all that's going to happen is that Mum and Dad are going to pull up in the car and jump out and fling their arms round me and laugh and cry and when they start getting cross about me running away from home I'll tell them about our exclusive use of Curly's mine for the next twenty-four hours with legal ownership of all the opals we find and they'll be so excited and overjoyed they'll do cartwheels and handstands and agree that me running away from home was the best thing that ever happened to us as a family.

The knot in his guts was still there.

He watched the Corolla skid to a stop.

His mouth was as dry as the dust swirling around him.

The doors of the Corolla flew open and Mum and Dad leapt out.

Keith's blood felt as though it was pumping around his body twice as fast as it usually did.

Maybe I'm not a worry wart, he thought hopefully, maybe I'm just excitable.

Mum and Dad were running towards him laughing and crying at the same time.

Keith decided to tell them about the mine straight away, just to be on the safe side.

'Mum,' he said, 'Dad . . .'

That was as far as he got because Mum and Dad swept him off his feet like two cyclones and hugged him and kissed him and gripped his head in their hands and buried their faces in his chest.

'Great news . . .' he said, but his voice was muffled by Mum's hair.

'. . . we've got . . .' he said, but the words were lost in Dad's armpit.

'. . . an opal mine,' he said, but neither of them could hear him because they were both talking at once.

'We thought you'd been kidnapped,' said Mum.

'We thought you'd got sick and collapsed on the way to school,' said Dad.

'We almost called the police,' said Mum.

'We almost called an ambulance,' said Dad.

'Then Tracy told us what had happened,' said Mum.

'Then Tracy told us where you'd gone,' said Dad.

Through the tangle of arms around him Keith saw something that made him stop trying to speak for several seconds.

Tracy, stepping out of the Corolla.

She gave him a nervous grin.

Then Keith realized Mum and Dad had stopped speaking too.

The lull before the storm, as Mr Gerlach always put

it when he stared quietly out the window for a few seconds before giving a noisy kid's ear a twist.

'Mum, Dad,' said Keith, 'before you get angry about me nicking off, I've got something to tell you.'

Mum and Dad gave each other a little glance.

'Son,' said Dad, his voice sounding a bit strange, 'we're not angry. We're just thankful you're OK.'

'We understand the stress you've been under, love,' said Mum.

She and Dad exchanged another glance.

At least they're not still avoiding looking at each other, thought Keith.

Then Mum and Dad noticed the store.

After they'd stared at it for a while and turned to Keith and seen the paint on his hands and clothes, their faces took on the expressions he knew so well.

Mum furrowed.

Dad drooped.

'Oh Keith,' said Mum.

'Why do you keep on doing this sort of thing?' said Dad.

'Because,' said Keith, 'I like it.'

He hadn't meant to say that.

Quickly he added what he had meant to say.

'I did it to get us an opal mine.'

He waited for Mum and Dad's delighted response.

It didn't come.

Give them time, thought Keith, they've had a long trip.

*

He gave them two hours.

During that time they spoke with the woman in the fluffy dressing-gown, moved into the caravan park's one overnight van, found a phone box, rang Tracy's parents, had showers, had something to eat, and asked Keith questions about his trip.

Keith kept his answers short.

Then Tracy told Keith about their trip. How the car had broken down and they'd had to wait seven hours for a man in dirty orange overalls to come and give them a tow back to his garage where he'd taken another four hours to fix the engine and had tried to sell them a microwave.

'That's Mick,' said Keith. 'I painted his mate Col's truck.'

Mum and Dad looked pained.

Tracy leaned over to Keith and whispered, 'The store looks great'.

He gave her a grateful grin.

But something was wrong.

Why did she look so anxious?

'Have you found any opal yet?' asked Tracy.

Keith decided everyone had had enough time to recover from the trip.

'That opal mine I mentioned before,' he said, 'it's ours for a whole day. We can dig up as many opals as we like and keep them.'

He waited for Mum and Dad to be overjoyed.

Mum and Dad exchanged a glance.

Mum put a hand on Dad's arm.

Silly me, thought Keith. Of course. They've had the

whole trip down here to get used to the fact that we're going to be fabulously wealthy and immensely happy.

Keith saw them swap another glance.

Look at the difference it's made to them, he thought.

Gazing into each other's eyes.

Touching each other.

'Keith,' said Dad, 'we're all going back to Orchid Cove first thing in the morning. You as well.'

Keith was sure he hadn't heard that right.

Maybe someone had just exploded some gelignite out on the diggings and the shock waves had distorted Dad's words.

Dad said it again.

Keith stared at him in disbelief.

Squinting at the road across a Tropical Parrot car bonnet for two days must have left Dad with temporary brain damage.

'Don't you understand,' Keith said to him, 'we've got our own opal mine. For a whole day. We'll never have money problems again. No more migraines or tummy upsets or arguments.'

Keith turned to Mum.

She'd understand.

'Keith,' she said, 'let's all go for a little walk and get some fresh air.'

Good idea, thought Keith. Fresh air'll help certain people's brains work properly.

They all stood up.

'Tracy,' said Mum, 'would you mind doing the washing-up while we have a little chat with Keith?'

Keith was about to protest. How dare they treat

Tracy, the person who'd helped them get to the brink of wealth and happiness, like a servant?

But before he could say anything Tracy said, 'Sure, no problem,' glancing anxiously at Mum and Dad.

Right, thought Keith angrily, wait till I get you two outside.

Outside it was dark.

They walked to the edge of the caravan park and stood staring at the mullock heaps, which were glowing faintly in the moonlight and looked to Keith like coconut macaroons.

Concentrate, Keith said to himself.

He knew it was very important to choose the right words, the words that would persuade Mum and Dad to stay for just one day so they could find the opals that would make them all happy for the rest of their lives.

But it was hard with Mum on one side and Dad on the other and both of them with an arm round his shoulders.

He didn't want to think, he just wanted to enjoy.

He decided to use telepathy and sent a double-strength message to both of them.

Change your minds.

'Keith,' said Dad softly, 'I wasn't being honest with you before.'

It's working, thought Keith joyfully.

'I wasn't either,' said Mum, 'we both weren't.'

'That's OK,' said Keith, 'I understand.'

'Keith,' said Mum, and there was a little sob in her voice which made Keith realize with a stab of fear that he didn't understand at all.

'Love,' she went on, 'Dad and I have decided to split up.'

'Not just in the shop,' said Dad, the sob in his voice too. 'For good.'

'But we want you to know,' said Mum, 'that we both love you as much now as we always have.'

'And we always will,' said Dad.

Keith knew what he should be saying.

That it would only take a day.

Half a day.

A couple of hours.

And that once they had the opals they could all stay together for ever.

But he couldn't get the words out through the numbness.

All he could do was stare at the mullock heaps, which were still glowing faintly in the moonlight and looked to Keith like graves.

TWELVE

Later, after Mum had whispered to Dad that Keith probably wanted to be by himself for a bit and they'd both hugged him and gone back to the caravan, Keith saw a torch beam moving towards him through the darkness.

For a moment Keith thought it was Mum come back to tell him they'd changed their minds.

It was Tracy.

'You OK?' she asked as she got nearer.

Keith turned and stared at the mullock heaps.

He'd never felt less OK in his life.

'Have they decided to do it?' Tracy asked softly. 'They were yakking on about it for hours in the car when they thought I was asleep. Are they gunna split up?'

Keith bit his lower lip hard so the pain was all he'd have to think about.

It didn't work.

He turned and glared at Tracy.

'One more day, that's all I needed,' he said bitterly. 'If you hadn't stuck your mug in I'd have been OK.'

In the glow from the torch he could see how much he'd hurt her.

Tough.

He didn't have time to worry about that.

He stared up at the black sky.

The stars glittered like a school bag full of opals emptied out on to a bank manager's desk.

It wasn't too late.

He turned and ran into the darkness.

The pickaxe he'd spotted while he was painting the store was still there, lying half under the verandah.

Keith grabbed it and hurried out into the diggings.

It wasn't easy moving fast. The rough ground was strewn with loose rocks and pitted with tyre tracks and fossickers' trenches.

He stumbled and if it hadn't been for Tracy hurrying behind him with the torch he'd have fallen down a shaft. She helped him up.

Which is the least she can do, thought Keith bitterly, after the damage she's done.

Then he saw it.

Keep Out.

Curly's mine.

He turned to Tracy, put his finger to his lips, crept up to the old caravan and listened.

Nothing.

He dropped the pickaxe into the dark shaft and uncoiled the wire from the winch. Tracy shone the torch on him while he slithered down, then threw it down to him.

He turned towards the tunnel.

'What about me?' hissed Tracy down the shaft.

Keith gave a long-suffering sigh and shone the torch up on her while she came down.

He had to admit, even though he didn't want to, that she was a good climber.

They went along the tunnel, the torch beam making the coloured bands of rock stand out like veins. The rusty metal poles holding the roof up threw eerie criss-cross patterns ahead of them.

Keith stopped and peered at a patch of rock.

He was sure he'd seen it glitter.

'If there was opal here,' said Tracy, 'they wouldn't have continued the tunnel on.'

That's just what he'd been thinking. Even though she didn't deserve it, he had to admit she was pretty smart.

Eventually they came to the end of the tunnel. The roof had gradually got lower and now they both had to crouch.

This is it, thought Keith, as he ran his hand over the different layers of rock.

They're in here somewhere.

He wished he'd asked Curly if the opals were in the smooth, hard rock or the rough, crumbly stuff.

Oh well, he'd soon find out.

He handed the torch to Tracy and gripped the pick-axe in both hands. Then he swung it as hard as he could. The metal point smashed into a layer of hard rock. Pain shot up Keith's arms and made his head ring.

He aimed the next swing at a crumbly layer. A shower of fragments sprayed over him but the pain in his arms was only half as bad.

He decided to concentrate on the crumbly layer.

*

Keith kept swinging until he couldn't feel the pick handle in his hands any more.

Then he stopped, gasping for breath, and looked closely at the rock wall. Nothing shimmered in the torchlight. No flashes of colour. No opals. Yet.

He flexed his shoulders to try to get rid of the ache, and got ready to swing the pickaxe again.

'Shall I have a go?' asked Tracy.

Keith opened his mouth to say yes, but that's not what came out.

'This isn't a tourist attraction,' he heard himself saying.

Half of him felt bad he was saying it and half of him felt good.

'That's why you're here, isn't it,' he went on, 'cause you want to travel and see the world, starting with a tour of the opal fields and a bit of opal mining?'

Tracy stared at him.

She looked even more hurt than before.

Then suddenly her eyes flashed angrily in the torchlight.

'The reason I'm here,' she said, 'is because after you nicked off your mum and dad were in such a hysterical mess they weren't thinking straight. They were gunna try and get here inland from Orchid Cove, down the stock route. People have died trying to drive down there in Corollas.'

Keith had a sudden vision of Mum and Dad sitting in their broken down car on the stock route, hungry lizards circling closer and closer.

'My dad was off working and my mum had Mrs

Newman's daughter Gail's kids,' Tracy was saying, 'so I was the only one around to navigate. It's not easy, navigating for someone who gets the trots as often as your old man. We spent half our time looking for thick scrub.'

Keith almost grinned, until he remembered that wasn't what he was meant to be feeling.

'You still didn't have to blab about what I was doing in the first place,' he said.

Tracy's shoulders slumped.

'I didn't want to,' she said, 'but when your mum and dad found you weren't at my place they went hysterical. They were gunna call the cops. There'd have been a nationwide search. Helicopters. Tracker dogs. TV. Reporters. You could have been shot or chewed up or featured on TV while you were crying or something.'

Keith looked at the concerned frown creasing her freckled forehead and suddenly he felt like swinging the pickaxe at his own bum.

How could he have been so scungy to the best mate he'd ever had?

'Sorry I've been carrying on like a wally,' he said.

'You mean a prawn,' she grinned.

'Yeah,' he said.

He told her he'd have another bash with the pickaxe, then she could have a go.

His second swing dislodged a rock the size of the big opal in Curly's store. He broke it in half with the pick, but it was just rock all the way through.

'Keith,' said Tracy softly, 'do you think this is gunna work?'

'It's got to,' he said, ''cause we haven't got any dynamite and Curly keeps his rock drill under the tinned fish.'

'No,' said Tracy, 'I mean even when we strike opal. Do you think the money's gunna make your mum and dad want to stay together?'

It's the fatigue, thought Keith, as he swung the pick-axe into the rock wall. She's been on the road for two days with Mum and Dad arguing all the time. No wonder she's over-tired and being a worry wart.

'My Auntie Fran and Uncle Leo split up,' said Tracy, 'and they were loaded. From Uncle Leo's mega insurance payout when he fell into the combine harvester.'

Don't listen to her, Keith told himself, or she'll have you being a worry wart too.

He moved his feet further apart and swung the pick-axe back as far as he could and smashed it into the rock.

Still no opals.

He swung it back again.

It hit something with a loud clang.

Tracy screamed.

Keith turned, and saw that the rusty iron roof support behind him was buckling in the middle. A gash of raw new metal was opening up as the support bent more and more out of shape.

Keith flung himself at it and tried to push it straight again.

Dust and small rocks showered onto him from the tunnel roof.

'Run,' he yelled at Tracy.

He could feel tremors and shudders running through the rock above his head. He pushed at the support with all his strength but even as he did he could feel that the force pressing down from above was a million times stronger than him.

The metal bent under his hands like a soggy chip and the last thing he saw, after Tracy had disappeared in a cloud of dust and falling rock, was a brief vision of Mum and Dad standing up on the surface, their weight added to the mass that was crushing him.

THIRTEEN

It was black with flashing colours.

Good grief, thought Keith, I'm looking at the biggest opal in the world.

Then he realized his eyes were closed.

He opened them.

Everything looked just as black, but without the colours.

He blinked a few times.

Still black.

For a moment he thought he was having the dream he'd once had where Elvis Presley crept into his bedroom and tried to smother him with a giant potato scallop.

But that couldn't be right because nobody was singing 'Are You Lonesome Tonight?'

Then he remembered where he was.

Lying in a mine with sharp rocks sticking into his back.

Perhaps they were opals.

He didn't give a stuff, they were still sharp.

He experimented with moving his arms and legs.

They all moved.

Several of them hurt, but not in a major way, not like when he'd fallen off his bike when he was seven and had ended up with eleven stitches in his leg and forty-seven in his trousers.

He groped around for any big rocks that might be lying on his chest which he hadn't felt yet on account of shock and having two T-shirts on.

There weren't any.

He sat up.

Colours exploded in front of his eyes as his head came into contact with something hard which felt like Col's truck reversing into him but which, Keith decided as he lay back down, was just a rock.

Best not to move.

Any number of giant slabs could be balanced on each other, just waiting for a nudge to come crashing down on him.

Then he remembered Tracy.

'Tracy!' he shouted.

He held his breath and listened.

Nothing.

Just the pounding of the veins in his head.

He remembered the last moment he'd seen her, standing as the dust came down, torn between getting away and staying to help.

He seemed to remember that she'd started to run.

Towards him.

Then nothing.

'Tracy!' he yelled.

He strained to hear a reply.

Even one muffled by tonnes of fallen rocks and opals.

Nothing.

He tried again.

He kept on trying till his voice was cracked and sobbing.

Then he stopped because he knew it was useless.

She couldn't hear him.

A long time later, when he'd finished crying, he hoped she hadn't felt any pain.

They'd talked about dying once, on the jetty near the fish co-op. Tracy had told him her approach was to stay cheerful because any day could be your last, specially if it was a day when the tuck shop had Mrs Reece's curry turnovers.

Keith wondered if he'd be able to stay cheerful now, trapped down here.

He wondered if he'd feel any pain, apart from the rocks sticking into his back.

He wondered how long it took twelve-year-old boys who were normally pretty healthy but who'd been under a lot of stress lately to starve to death.

Then he made himself stop wondering.

Six months ago, on a drizzly street in South London, he'd decided he wasn't going to spend the rest of his life being a misery guts and a worry wart.

Think positive.

When I get out of this, Keith thought, I'm going to put a brass plate on Curly's store dedicating the paint job to Tracy. And I'm going to write to Col and get him to put one on his truck painting.

Then he had an even better idea.

He'd do a special painting, just for Tracy. A huge painting, on hundreds of pieces of plywood stuck together, of her in all the places in the world she'd wanted to visit.

Tracy admiring the view at a campsite in Alaska. Tracy waterskiing in Venice. Tracy climbing a mountain range in Egypt. Tracy checking out all the flat but interesting places in Peru. Tracy visiting all the traditional villages in remote valleys untouched by the modern world around Melbourne.

It would be the most fabulous painting anyone had ever painted.

Keith lay there in the dark and he could see every detail, even though his eyes had filled with tears again.

Because she'd still be dead.

A painting wouldn't bring her back.

He couldn't bring her back any more than he could make Mum and Dad fall in love again.

He let the hot tears run down his cheeks even though he knew he'd regret it later when he was suffering from dehydration.

After a while he knew something else.

If it'd bring Tracy back to life, he'd help Mum and Dad pack their bags so they could split up tomorrow.

Even if it meant Dad going to live in an Alaskan campsite and only seeing him every other weekend when the ice had thawed.

Or Mum going to live up an Egyptian mountain and only seeing her every other weekend when the camels were running.

Suddenly Keith heard himself shouting it, screaming it at the top of his voice, so they'd know.

'Split up!'

'Split up!'

'Split up!'

He kept on shouting it until his throat was raw and he'd run out of tears.

And until something had happened that made him suddenly go silent and strain every muscle in his body to hear better.

A familiar voice, faint and grumpy, coming from somewhere close.

'Keep the noise down, you dopey mongrel.'

FOURTEEN

Keith sat up and banged his head again.

He didn't care.

'Tracy,' he screamed, hoarse with delight as well as all the shouting he'd just done.

'I'm over here,' she mumbled. 'Put a sock in it, I've got a headache.'

Keith felt himself go weak with relief. Before he could move towards her voice, a blinding light smacked him in the eyes.

It was so bright that at first Keith thought it was a rescue light attached to a giant drill that had drilled through the rock to them without him noticing because he'd been so busy yelling.

But when he peeped through his fingers he saw it was just the torch.

Holding it, sprawled on the ground nearby, one hand over her eyes, was Tracy.

'Are you OK?' he croaked.

She was covered in dust, and the rip in the knee of her jeans that she'd been carefully cultivating was about three times as long as it had been, and she had a big bruise over one eye.

'I think I was knocked out,' said Tracy. 'In fact I'm sure I was 'cause it happened to me once in softball and I dreamed about Peru that time as well. What about you?'

'I wasn't too good a minute ago,' said Keith, 'but now I'm great.'

They compared bruises and Keith told her he'd thought she'd been killed and she said it'd take more than a softball bat or sixty thousand tonnes of rock to do that.

She told him she'd thought he'd been a goner too, for about four seconds until he'd started making more noise than Ryan Garner's brother's garage band.

They grinned and hugged each other.

Then they realized what they were doing and both gave in to a sudden urge to study their surroundings.

It took Keith a few moments to realize that the space they were in, which was about the size of the average store room in the average fish and chip shop but with a lower ceiling, was actually the end of the tunnel.

Blocking the way out was a wall of fallen rocks.

'Let's see if we can get through,' said Tracy.

They hurled themselves at the rocks and clawed and dug with their hands until they were exhausted.

They moved three small ones.

Which allowed them to see even bigger ones behind.

This is hopeless, thought Keith. Half the tunnel could be collapsed.

He didn't say anything because he didn't want to depress Tracy.

'Half the tunnel's probably collapsed,' said Tracy.

Keith said it probably wasn't quite that bad.

'What's the time?' asked Tracy.

Keith looked at his watch.

All he could see was Mongolian Beige.

'They must have noticed we're missing by now,' he said. 'Let's try shouting in case they're up top.'

He took a deep breath.

'Help!' he yelled as loudly as he could, hoping his lungs didn't rupture with the effort. 'Help!'

Tracy put her hand on his arm and told him how her Uncle Wal had told her that people always took more notice if you shouted Fire.

'Fire!' they yelled. 'Fire!'

Then Tracy remembered that Aunty Cath had pointed out that in their neck of the woods there was one word that always turned people's heads more than Fire.

'Rain!' shouted Tracy. 'Rain!'

Keith joined in and they shouted it till he thought his throat was bleeding.

Then they listened.

Nothing.

'They can't hear us,' croaked Keith. 'Must be cause they're making so much racket up top getting all the rescue equipment into position.'

Tracy agreed that must be the reason.

They sat and stared at the pattern the torch beam made on the wall of fallen rocks. On the ground Keith noticed a flat piece of metal about as big as a pizza box that had been wedged between the top of the support and the roof of the tunnel.

He caught himself wondering if he'd ever have another pizza.

Think positive.

He wished he felt as confident about the rescue equipment as he'd sounded.

Think positive.

He glanced at Tracy.

Good old Tracy, he said to himself, she hasn't had a negative thought in her whole life.

'If they don't find us,' said Tracy quietly, 'in two hundred years we'll be dust and nobody'll ever know we were here.'

Keith stared at her, shocked.

What we need, he thought, is something to take our minds off things.

Then he had an idea.

'Do you remember what Mr Gerlach said once, about what people do when they want to live for ever? They have their portraits painted.'

Now it was Tracy's turn to stare at him.

Keith picked up the piece of metal and dusted it off.

'This'll do for a canvas,' he said, 'now all I need is some paint.'

He remembered they were down a mine.

I'm going stupid, he thought. The oxygen down here must be running out and starving my brain.

Then he saw what Tracy was doing and decided her brain must be short of oxygen too.

She was on her knees, scooping dust into a pile.

When she'd finished she crouched by the opposite wall.

'OK,' she said, turning away and putting one hand

over her eyes and pointing to the pile of dust with the other, 'pee on it.'

'Don't move,' said Keith, 'I've only got the freckles to do.'

He dabbed on some freckles as lightly as he could.

It wasn't bad, this dust paint, even if it did pong a bit. It was very similar to the dull red anti-rust paint, only grittier.

And even though he hadn't done finger painting since he was three, the result wasn't looking too bad at all.

'Finished,' he said.

Tracy got up from where she'd been sitting holding the torch half on her and half on him, and took the piece of metal.

She held it out, shone the torch on it, and studied it seriously.

Oh no, thought Keith, she doesn't like it. I'm stuck down a mine with an angry critic.

She gave a big grin.

'Ripper,' she said. 'It's even better than the cane toad. Thanks.'

Keith glowed.

'When we get out,' he said, 'I'll frame it for you.'

'If we get out,' she said.

'OK,' said Keith quickly, 'now it's my turn.'

He took the piece of metal and turned it over. The other side was mottled with rust stains and mineral deposits that had leached out of the rock.

If he painted his face on it he really would look like a cane toad.

His shoulders slumped.

Tracy shone the torch over the ground and around the walls.

'How about that?' she said.

Keith peered into the ring of the torch beam.

Against the side wall of the tunnel was a sheet of corrugated iron about half as tall as him.

He tried to pull it away but it was fixed to the rock.

'Must be to stop subsidence,' said Keith. 'Doesn't matter, it's OK where it is.'

He crouched down, dusted it off with one of his T-shirts and got to work.

It wasn't easy, he discovered, painting yourself from memory, specially if you'd never painted yourself before even with a mirror.

It took ages, with a lot of thinking and trying to remember what he looked like in the photo on the shelf in the living room at home.

He hoped Tracy wasn't getting bored.

He could hear her behind him, scraping rocks.

'Don't hurt your hands tunnelling,' he said, 'It's a waste of time. Wait for them to come to us.'

'I'm not tunnelling,' she said, 'I'm writing.'

Keith turned and saw that she'd scratched a word onto the end wall of the tunnel with a rock.

Peru.

'Peru?' said Keith.

'It's a reminder,' she said quietly. 'For later on. When we get weak. So we don't give up too easily.'

Keith stared at it.

Then he finished his painting.

'What do you think?' he said.

Tracy looked at it thoughtfully.

'Looks better than the Corolla,' she said, and gave him a little grin. 'It's great. It's got that expression you get when you're thinking. The one that makes you look like that guy on telly.'

Keith didn't ask which guy in case she meant Bugs Bunny.

'There is just one thing, though,' she went on. 'You look about seven.'

Keith stared at the painting.

She was right.

The face, the hair, the expression in the eyes.

It was a little kid.

Why had he done that?

He thumped the corner of the corrugated iron with his fist in frustration. Dust fell away from around the edges. And suddenly Keith felt something he hadn't felt before.

A draught.

Coming from behind the sheet of iron.

He grabbed the piece of metal with Tracy's portrait on it, wedged it behind the sheet of iron, and twisted as hard as he could.

'Hey,' said Tracy, 'don't do that, it doesn't matter about you looking young, it's good. And you're scratching mine.'

Rusty screws snapped and popped out and the iron sheet tore away from the rock.

Keith and Tracy stared at what was behind it.

A tunnel.

It was narrow but it was big enough to crawl along.

'Come on,' said Keith.

He went first with the torch.

The rock floor of the tunnel was murder on their knees, but it didn't matter because after they went round a curve they could see grey light up ahead.

A few minutes later they crawled out into the bottom of a shaft.

A wire ladder with bits of plastic pipe for rungs hung down from the top. They flung themselves up it without stopping for breath and suddenly they were out in the open air, lying on a mullock heap, gasping and laughing, the sky above them streaked with dawn light.

Keith heard a generator chug into life over on the next heap and looked across and saw a crowd of people standing around the shaft to Curly's mine. They were silhouetted against the rising sun, but he could make out Mum and Dad.

'Let's go and surprise them,' he said, getting up.

'Wait,' said Tracy. 'I've got something to show you.'

Keith saw that she was clutching the piece of metal with her portrait on it to her chest.

Even as he was trying to find a way of telling her how good that made him feel without sounding mushy, Tracy put her hand into her pocket and pulled out a dirty rock the size of a medium flathead fillet, battered.

'It's the one I was writing with,' she said. 'Didn't know what it was till the end broke off.'

As she held it out to him, the first weak rays of the

sun hit it and colours flashed out of it just like they had out of the opal in Curly's store.

Except, thought Keith as he gazed at it, the colours in Curly's opal were watercolours and these are oils.

Cobalt, vermilion, magenta, that sort of stuff.

He looked at Tracy holding the painting and the opal, and suddenly he knew what he had to do.

He grabbed the torch and ran to the shaft and started climbing down the ladder.

'No!' shouted Tracy, 'Don't be a dill! Come back!'

The tunnel was as hard on his knees as it had been before, and when Keith staggered back into the cavity they'd just escaped from he heard the roar of drills and saw that the roof was trembling and dust was falling all around him.

He didn't care.

There, on the ground in front of him, was what he'd come for.

As he picked it up, the torchlight and the tears in his eyes made it flash momentarily with a million points of coloured light.

Even at that instant, when it looked like a dazzling sheet of opal instead of a piece of corrugated iron, he could still see, clearly, himself.

FIFTEEN

From the moment Keith climbed out of the shaft, it was chaos.

There were faces all around him, and lights, and voices all speaking at once.

Mum and Dad were hugging him and crying all over him.

He tried to tell them to be careful of his painting because corrugated iron rusted easily, but they weren't listening.

He saw the Corolla parked nearby, headlights aimed at the shaft, so he went and put the painting in the boot.

Then two men in white overalls led him over to a bright yellow tent sitting next to a red helicopter.

Tracy came out of the tent and saw him and broke into a huge relieved grin.

'Jeez you're a prawn,' she said and hugged him so tight Keith could feel his face going as red as the helicopter, partly from embarrassment and partly because she was squeezing all his blood up into his head.

He was glad when he got into the tent and discovered that the two men in overalls were doctors. At least doctors were used to that sort of physical contact.

While the doctors checked him over they explained they were from a nearby coal mine, only four hundred kilometres away, and that they often came over to patch people up and do a bit of fossicking.

Then he found himself back outside with a blanket round his shoulders and hot drink in his hands and all sorts of people he'd seen on the diggings crowding round him.

The ultraviolet man touched his blanket for luck.

A middle-aged woman in a cardigan and gumboots who Keith didn't recognize until he saw that she was wearing a fluffy dressing-gown underneath, took his photo.

The ex-Department of Main Roads post painter offered him a beer until the woman in the fluffy dressing-gown told him to stop it.

Then Curly, bald head and wrinkled face looking strangely off-white even in the yellow rays of the morning sun, gripped his arm and took him to one side.

'Sorry I damaged your mine,' said Keith.

'Don't worry about that,' said Curly, 'and anything you found is yours, no questions.'

He leant closer with an anxious glance around to make sure no one was listening and Keith could see that he was going to ask at least one question.

'That tunnel you escaped through,' muttered Curly, 'the one that runs from my claim into the, um, claim next to mine, has anyone asked you about it?'

Keith was just about to say no when they were interrupted by the roar of a motor bike. The man with the beard and the European accent got off and came over to Curly and handed him a wooden sign daubed with faded red lettering.

It said *Tresspassers Will Be Stabbed*.

Curly went even more off-white.

The man took the sign back and handed Curly some Jehovah's Witness pamphlets.

Then Mum and Dad appeared with Tracy.

Keith saw that Mum and Dad were holding hands.

'Come on love,' said Mum to Keith, 'let's all go for a little walk.'

The sun was above the horizon as they walked slowly between the mullock heaps.

Keith tried to concentrate on the warmth on his face so he'd forget the knot in his guts.

It was no good.

Every time he glanced at Mum and Dad holding hands it got tighter.

Then Tracy spoke.

'Shall I go first, Mr and Mrs Shipley?' she asked.

'All right love,' said Mum, 'you go first.'

'Keith,' said Tracy, giving him a big grin, 'this is for you.'

She held out the opal.

'I know I found it,' she went on, 'but we wouldn't be here if it wasn't for you nicking off, and we wouldn't have been down that mine if it wasn't for you painting the store, and I wouldn't have been writing stuff on the wall if it wasn't for you keeping my spirits up, so it's really yours.'

She put it into his hand.

Keith looked at it for a long time because he wanted to choose exactly the right words for what he was going to say.

He looked at Tracy and his guts tingled so much that they almost unknotted.

'Jeez you're a dopey mongrel,' he said, grinning. 'And if you don't send me a postcard from Peru I'll come over there and boot you up the bum.'

He put the opal back into her hand.

Dad cleared his throat.

'Keith,' he said, 'before you react hastily, wait till you understand why Tracy's making such a generous offer.'

He cleared his throat again.

Oh no, thought Keith, Dad's got to have his tonsils out and it's to pay for the operation.

But he knew that wasn't the real reason.

'Keith,' said Dad, 'Mum and me have talked about it for most of the night, and we've decided not to split up.'

'We've decided to stay together,' said Mum. 'For your sake. We've talked about it and we're determined to make it work.'

'And the opal is to help with the financial problems,' said Tracy.

Keith stared out across the mullock heaps, which were glowing in the morning sun and looked like mounds of gold.

He took a deep breath of cool, clear morning air.

This was the moment he'd come halfway across

Queensland for, halfway around the world really, and he'd never dreamt it would be like this.

But it was, and he knew exactly what he was going to do.

He took another deep breath and even though he felt sadder than he ever had before, the knot in his guts was suddenly gone.

He turned back to Mum and Dad. They were both smiling as hard as they could, but Mum's forehead was still furrowed and Dad's mouth was still droopy.

'That is what you want, isn't it love?' asked Mum in a shaky voice.

Keith looked at them both and slowly shook his head.

SIXTEEN

Keith peered across Trafalgar Square into the late morning fog.

Everything was grey. Grey buildings. Grey shops. Grey cars.

Nelson's Column was grey, looming up into the grey London sky.

Keith grinned.

What a great day.

He pulled Tracy's letter from his pocket and read it for the nineteenth time since it had arrived at Dad's place that morning.

Dear Keith,

Ripper, eh? Only another ten days and I'll be there. It's great you've got two bedrooms now cause that means I won't have to pay camping ground fees and I'll have more opal money left for checking out London.

My folks have said I might be able to stay for a seventh week! They're really rapt cause the new roof is on now and their bedroom doesn't leak any more.

I had a lend of a book on Peru. It still looks pretty interesting, but not as interesting as the London Underground. What happens if a train breaks down? Do they have toilets down there? Mrs Newman reckons underground trains make your feet swell. Can't wait.

Say g'day to your folks from me. It must be exciting, having a mum who's a Parking Inspector.

See you soon.

Love Tracy.

PS. Mr Gerlach put your cane toad painting on the front of the school magazine.

PPS. When you said you painted your Dad's new shop fourteen colours, was that inside as well or just outside?

Keith put the letter back in his pocket and looked at his watch. It had been running a bit slow ever since he'd put it in the turps to get rid of the Mongolian Beige.

Eleven thirty-eight.

Or thereabouts.

Heaps of time.

He'd got four days to finish off painting his bedrooms before Tracy arrived. His room at Mum's place was just about finished except for the rainforest mural on the ceiling. And all he had to do to finish off his room at Dad's place was to put a second coat of Tropical Parrot on the wardrobe and add the Hot Sunflower speed stripes.

Keith climbed the steps of the National Gallery and went inside.

He walked slowly through the rooms, lingering in front of his favourite paintings.

As usual he didn't spend long looking at the one called *Giovanni Arnolfini and His Wife* because the man and woman reminded him of Mum and Dad before they cheered up.

Still, he thought, it's interesting that people married

the wrong people even five hundred and sixty years ago.

He noticed that the walls in one of the Early Italian rooms had been repainted.

Satin Finish Eggshell Enamel.

Not bad.

Keith wandered on through the gallery, smiling as he thought about bringing Tracy here.

After she'd checked out all the paintings, specially the Rembrandt *Self Portrait* which looked a bit like a cane toad, and he'd shown her the Flemish rooms, which desperately needed some Celery Green around the windows, he'd tell her his secret ambition.

That one day his work would be on these walls.

'Inside the picture frames or around them?' she'd ask with a grin.

He'd grin back and give a shrug.

Didn't matter.

He was a painter, not a worry wart.

Morris Gleitzman
Puppy Fat

'What section do you want to advertise in? Toys? Sporting Equipment? Computers and Video Games?' The woman in the newspaper office took off her glasses and polished them on her cardigan. 'What are you advertising?'

'My parents,' said Keith.

Keith's worried. Can two single parents with saggy tummies, wobbly bottoms and dodgy legs ever find happiness? Not a chance, decides Keith, unless he can get them into shape. Just as well Tracy the mountaineer and Aunty Bev the beautician are arriving from Australia . . .

The brilliantly funny sequel to *Misery Guts* and *Worry Warts*.

Morris Gleitzman
Blabber Mouth

Two hours ago, when I walked into this school for the first time, the sun was shining, the birds were singing, and, apart from a knot in my guts the size of Tasmania, life was great. Now here I am, locked in a stationery cupboard. I wish those teachers would stop shouting at me to come out.

Hiding in cupboards is one way of dealing with your problems. Especially when you've just stuffed a frog into Darryn Peck's mouth.

But Rowena Batts has a bigger problem. Her dad. How can she tell him that his shirts, and his singing voice, are wrecking her life? It's not easy – especially when you can't speak . . .

'A wonderful novel.' *School Librarian*

'Hysterically funny.' *Books for Keeps*

Morris Gleitzman
Two Weeks with the Queen

Dear Your Majesty the Queen,

I need to speak to you urgently about my brother Luke. He's got cancer and the doctors in Australia are being really slack. If I could borrow your top doctor for a few days I know he/she would fix things up in no time. Of course Mum and Dad would pay his/her fares even if it meant selling the car or getting a loan. Please contact me at the above address urgently.

Yours sincerely

Colin Mudford

P.S. This is not a hoax. Ring the above number and Aunty Iris will tell you. Hang up if a man answers.

If you want something done properly – go straight to the top!

Getting the Queen to help won't be easy. But if she can't help – who can?

'One of the best books I've ever read. It's funny, moving and it handles difficult subjects with skill and great respect. I'm glad I read it. I wish that I had written it.'
Paula Danziger

'A remarkably exciting, moving and funny book.'
Children's Books of the Year 1989

'A marvellous book – funny and wise.'
Books for Keeps

'A gem of a book.'
Stephanie Netall, *The Guardian*

Morris Gleitzman titles
available from Macmillan

The prices shown below are correct at the time of going to press. However, Macmillan Publishers reserve the right to show new retail prices on covers which may differ from those previously advertised.
